WINTER

MIST RIDERS
BOOK TWO

Stella Fitzsimons

BUTTERFLY ELECTRIC PRESS

WINTER

The Chronicles of Luna Mae

Chapter 1

THE BORGO WAS SMALL enough to fit in my palm. Even at full maturity, borgos rarely grew much bigger than a teddy bear and this one was still a baby.

Nanya squeaked when I gently touched her little white nose with a knuckle. I smiled into her big, dark eyes and played with her soft, pointy ears.

"Here we are," Gram said, setting down a tray of coconut cookies and tea. "I'll miss this sweet little fluff baby so much," she said. "Such an innocent soul."

Borgos were now rare in the Deep Down, as precious and dear as one's own child. Petting them was therapeutic—their fur was so warm and soft like cotton candy. The legend was that once upon a time there were enough of the little fluffs to fill a small town, but now so few were born that each birth became celebrated. Looking into the eyes of a newborn

Borgo was as soul touching and exalted as the discovery of a black pearl in the Arctic Ocean.

Nanya was born prematurely and had little chance of survival unless an experienced witch dedicated herself day and night to nursing the fragile preemie. Gram happily volunteered and three months later, baby borgo was strong enough for a return to the Deep Down.

The baby fluff yawned in my palm. She wagged her short tail, made a low, playful growl, then leapt off my palm with blurring speed and landed on Gram's Christmas tree.

Her mouth snapped wide open as if her head had split in half, baring long, sharp teeth that clearly didn't belong on such a tiny body.

Green needles went flying as the borgo chewed on both tree and ornaments like a woodchipper, shredding them to pieces.

I gasped. I knew borgos were far from the harmless creatures they appeared to be, yet to witness the sudden damage such a tiny one could cause left me stunned.

"There, there," Grandma scolded. With a wave of her hand, she released a pale spark of energy to immobilize the mischievous fluff. "You are quite the naughty girl," Gram whispered, lifting Nanya out of the tree.

"You have spoiled her, same as you did me," I said, still in awe of the stark transformation that had taken place in front of my eyes.

Sitting in the coziness of Gram's living room had

a calming effect. I'd been on the verge of hyperventilating since I boarded the plane to Portland after that awkward conversation with Winter at the airport.

I remained defiant in his presence. I told him I would no longer be a part of the whole deadly madness of his bullshit rivalry with Chaos, but his words began to sink in on the airplane. The Immortals' plan for world dominion, Düsternis's deceit, the scheming certainty of Chaos. All of it. Could I even pretend to harbor an illusion of keeping my distance? Would I ever again be able to lead any semblance of a normal life?

"You look depleted, my dear. I know that look, it's the look of a witchling in need of phosphorus. There's a new seafood place down on 12th Street. It's charming, right on the water, and they're open on Christmas Day. I checked. They're doing anything they can to bring in more business."

Grandma's voice reached me as if from far away. I tried to smile. "Just tired, Gram," I said as I picked up my cup of tea.

"Oh, my weary little traveler, don't you know you can't hide things from your grandmother?"

I knew. My grandma could sense my every mood, feel my every pain, whether it be physical or emotional. There was no one I loved more or trusted more. She looked older—the gray in her hair had started taking over, age spots stained her hands, and the wrinkles on her forehead pinched a permanent V between her benevolent eyebrows.

I didn't want to blame her for all I had learned. Yet, there was no way around the facts. We had opened our presents and had our traditional Christmas breakfast of eggs benedict, turkey sausage and gingerbread pancakes. Nanya decimating the tree ornaments had only added to the charm of a successful holiday morning.

I sipped my tea, then put the cup down. "An Immortal told me he's watched me since I was a child. Do you know anything about that, Gram?"

All color left Grandma's face as her eyes narrowed. A small sigh escaped her lips. "I hoped he would wait. I never thought he'd come back so soon."

"Come back? You knew about it all? You're part of this?"

"Sophie, I ask you to process this, slowly. There are no easy answers. My own understanding changed with time. I learned more along the way. This is not a man who left anything to chance."

"Why did you allow it? Why would my parents allow it?"

Grandma put her hands together to stop them from shaking. "Your mother had no choice. Your father... the man you know as your father, he didn't want anything to do with it. A month after they took you in, he left."

The world I knew melted around me. "What do you mean... *took me in?*"

Gram closed her eyes. "When you were a baby, the Immortal, Winter, arrived at our door, holding you in his arms. He implored us to raise you as our own, to keep you safe."

My eyes watered. "I'm not your flesh and blood?"

"Honey, love is beyond flesh. You could not be more of my heart since the moment I laid eyes on you. Your mother adored you to the moon and back. She'd have given her life for you and done it with a smile."

I turned to the window. Snow had fallen during the night, turning the backyard cotton white. In the distance, the Columbia River was restless. Fishing vessels swayed in the gray blue waters. Everything felt somehow connected to the anguish in Gram's voice.

"And yet my mother is gone. Was what happened to her because of me?"

"A child is never to blame for the things bad men do. I found you that day. You were hidden in the basement cloaked in your mother's most powerful wards. Your mother had put up a hell of a fight. The place was a mess, but you were safe. That's all she wanted. She won that day, Sophie. What happened to her was not a tragedy. It was a victory."

"I was four at the time... I should be able to remember it."

"Her protection was complete. She cloaked both your body and mind."

Grandma wavered. Tears gathered. My worst fears were confirmed. Mind cloaking often came at a cost. I was the reason my mother had been trapped inside her own mind. "Was it Winter who had come for me?"

"Winter? No, child. He would not harm you. He was furious when he found out. Devastated, even. He tried everything to bring your mother back. He needed to know who was after you. Only she could tell him. I had to plead for him to relocate us, so we could remain together. That's when we came to Astoria and assumed these new identities. If he wanted you back, he could have easily taken you."

I took a breath to process. "So, we're not from Oregon?"

"You're from Oregon. I'm from the tidal marshes of the Georgia coast."

Gram patted down the front of her dress, oddly calm, as if relieved to have finally set down the weight of her secrets.

"I am from nowhere it seems. From nowhere and from no one," I said. "Grandma, I love you, but I have been a curse to your family."

"Sophie, never forget that a curse is a spell of sorts," Gram said with a reassuring pat on my knee. "And spells are the family business. You are as far from a curse as could be possible."

"Did Winter ever mention how and why he had taken an interest in me in the first place?"

Grandma shook her head. "He barely spoke of it. All he would say is that he'd given an oath to your family to keep you safe."

Huh, the bastard knew my real family. Yet another lie.

"Why this family? Why did he bring me to you?"

"Because you were a lunar witch and he was acquainted with my great-great-great grandmother. They were on friendly terms and she owed him."

OMG. "You don't mean they were... involved?"

"Oh dear, no, nothing like that. Winter saved her from certain death when she was a captive of the Grand Magistrate and the Seventh Council. It wasn't the first time he protected a lunar witch. He has always been sympathetic toward our kind. I don't believe he would ever hurt a witch."

"You have too much faith in people."

Concern sparked in Gram's eyes. "Has something happened?"

"Yes, Gram, something has," I said, trying not to come undone. "Things are happening. And I wish they would just stop. I have my own plans."

"Why don't you tell me what happened?"

Where to begin? "Have you heard of an Immortal named Chaos?"

Gram considered the name for a few moments. "No, I can't say that I have. I know very little about Immortals."

Consider yourself lucky, Gram.

"Do you know what a Shadow Warrior is?"

"Shadow Warriors?" Gram repeated. "What is this all about?"

"Right. Well, this Chaos guy and Winter are Shadows, on top of expert assassins, which also means they have the ability to kill each other, despite being Immortals." I chuckled as I realized the depths of my own ignorance. "I actually threw myself between them and saved Winter's life. It was before I knew the truth about Winter's deceit. In retrospect, I should have let Chaos take his head. All my problems would have been solved."

I quickly explained about Chaos, the morphs and how Winter had used me, leaving out the bits about me being a mist rider and the Immortals' plan to take over the Deep Down and, eventually, the world. There was no reason to alarm her before I knew more myself. Grandma would turn eighty in spring. I wouldn't drag her into this doomsday mess if I could help it.

"I wish you'd have come to me," she said pensively.

"I had Faion by my side. Faion Trice. You know him, don't you? He says you know his grandmother."

"Faion? Celia's grandson? How did that come about?"

I shrugged. "He's a diviner. He knew I needed help."

Grandma searched for an appropriate response. This was too much information to dump on her all at once. Of course, she needed to process. Still, the silence became awkward as the seconds raced past. A gnawing suspicion grew that she might be keeping things from me even now.

I gulped down the last of my tea. "Just how many magics are there in Astoria anyway?"

"Sounds like you know all of them."

Life in Astoria had always been simple, peaceful, even idyllic. The most excitement the town had ever known was back in the eighties and early nineties when they filmed both *Goonies* and *Free Willy* here. And that had happened years before I was born.

Astoria was just a quaint town on the Columbia River with a population of ten thousand. Among that population were two non-practicing lunar witches and two diviners who had long since left the Deep Down behind.

This time, it was Gram who broke the silence. "I suppose you'll be visiting your mother, then."

"Yes," I said, feeling fatigued. "Tomorrow morning. With Faion."

It was hard to believe it had been three days since we arrived home. I hadn't spoken to him at all during that time. I could use a bit of his restless energy and frenetic sense of humor.

Gram's shoulders hunched slightly as she sighed. "Will you take Nanya with you? It's time she rejoined her family."

I glanced at the tiny borgo asleep on the couch. "I don't know," I said. "That's a terrifying little creature."

"You can't be serious."

"I kind of am."

"You're just being silly," Gram said as she watched Nanya sleep. The little fluff's breathing brought calm smiles to our faces.

"I'll get her home," I promised.

"Be careful along the way," Gram said, her mood darkening.

"Aren't I always?" Not so long ago that would have rung true.

Gram wiped her mouth with her hand and nodded. "You really should stay for New Year's." This was the fourth time she mentioned New Year's. It had become a sad refrain.

"Gram, you know I can't. I have the apartment to clean. I have to pack, sell the furniture, turn in my keys, say my goodbyes to friends and get on a plane to Europe."

"I know, sweetie. It was just a grandmother's wish. How about I visit you in San Diego instead? I could use a change of scenery."

I gathered up our cups to take to the kitchen. Halfway there, I stopped.

"Would you trust Winter?" I turned back. "You know, if you were me?"

Grandma's voice came out weak, uncertain. "What does a forgotten old lady know? I guess I never really knew him well enough to judge."

"Just trust your gut," I insisted.

Grandma took her time, tapping her nails on her lap. "Yes, I think I would. I would trust him. I've seen the worry in his eyes, and he is steadfast. Not many men are these days."

I did not possess the energy to describe for her all the various lies and manipulations orchestrated by her Mr. Steadfast over the previous months.

"I'll take some air," I shouted from the kitchen. I would offer to help with the dirty dishes, but I knew Gram would turn me down anyway.

I stepped out into a crisp winter breeze. I was taking a walk as much to allow Gram a chance to peer deep into her orb as I was to clear my head of all my fractured memories and unwanted destinies.

It was Christmas in Astoria. Those were once charmed words. Step-by-step I tried to remember my town, my home, the heart at the center of the girl I had once been.

Chapter 2

Faion's eyes widened as he took in the thundering twin waterfalls. On either side of the main falls, lesser streams splashed over the basalt cliffs like a million sparkling tears running down the rocky, green plateau.

In the river basin at the base stood a twenty-foot, diamond-shaped rock that remained dry despite its location at the roaring center of the perpetual onslaught of falling waters.

This was the gate to the Deep Down.

Magic filled the air, fortifying our etheric fields and warming our skin. We waded out through the river and into the hissing mist at the foot of the falls.

I fought to control my own hissing current of magic. Its power was hard to resist so near the Deep Down, the primal source of witchcraft, sorcery and all things supernatural found on the planet. Efforts to suppress my impulses caused a deep physical ache and a gnawing mental anguish.

Fighting to hold ourselves together, Faion and I tightened our fists and focused our intent. Nanya, on the other hand, seemed perfectly calm, having traveled through this gate not long ago. Her miniature head stuck out of my jacket pocket to watch our struggles with great curiosity.

Faion gripped my hand, then placed his other hand flat on the dry rock face within the surrounding mist.

"Succumb," he ordered the gate.

The magic word hissed in and out of our mouths, creating a chorus of echoes as we felt a feverish energy rising all around us.

The ground shook under our feet as the falls suddenly enveloped us, cloaking us completely from the outside world. We were quickly sucked into a silver crease of light that cut through the center of the rock.

The rock crackled and slammed shut in a sudden *whoosh*. The falls were gone and with them the sun. Now we stood in a dark corridor—the deafening rush of the falls had been reduced to a distant hum or perhaps just an auditory memory from another world.

Nanya squealed enthusiastically, racing up onto my shoulder.

"Furby's all jacked up for home," Faion said.

When he went to pet the Borgo, Nanya growled and bared a line of sharp, serrated teeth.

Faion retrieved his hand. "Little diva's crazy."

"That's just her way of playing."

"Right. Bet she's a real popular play date," Faion said.

"Dude," I said, amused.

A soft lavender glow sparked forth revealing a long path ahead. We walked down the tunnel, marveling at the elaborate marks on the walls—enchanted scripts, glyphs and cryptic runes that blazed fire red before fading away as we passed.

I had no training in archaic iconography, but Faion was able to use his divining knowledge to read some of the script before it vanished.

Bear your transgressions
Fortify the power
Walk within the light

At the end of the tunnel, we came upon a circle. An elaborate pattern of oversized flowers and branches decorated the stone floor. Five paths coiled away from the loop like the spokes of a wheel.

The Deep Down was an intricate labyrinth of Minoan proportions with the ability to restructure itself when under attack, almost like the reshuffling of a deck of cards. Anyone unfamiliar with its transposing design principles guided by magic and ritual would never find their way in—or out.

Faion and I took the path to our left until we came upon a narrow staircase. A cherry red door stood ajar at the top.

We climbed the stairs. A cold gust rifled through the open

door, blowing back my hair. A thin layer of frost slicked the surface of the door. It was all an illusion, I knew, a test of some sort. We could not just walk through the door. If we did, we very well might be instantly fried.

My eyes closed as I began to chant one of the first spells I had ever learned, a simple yet powerful incantation capable of opening most gates in our enchanted world while shattering all involved wards back to their primal elements.

I spoke the words slowly, my voice in a lower register than usual.

"Through earth and through sky, free my way or a price you will pay."

The frame of the door lit up with a golden glow. The shimmering light spread everywhere, pulsing under our feet and chasing away the frost.

A realm of unmatched beauty stretched open as the wards guarding the door surrendered and fled. Tall trees covered with spring green foliage traced the perimeters of two wild parklands so vast they could have been nature reserves in the basic world.

Between them, a wide trail rolled down an easy slope to a small town of brick roads and tile roofs as colorful as any fairy-tale village.

The air was ripe with aromas from flower gardens and steaming casseroles. The sky was a clear azure, the sunlight warm and welcoming.

"How much I've missed this place," I whispered,

breathing deeply.

"I heard that," Faion said, rubbing his hands together. "Now let's go find that food."

There was a lot more to the Deep Down than the name suggested. The basic portals all led to the underground realm but once there, taking certain paths led to towns and forests under the sun, concealed by enchanted domes of energy that kept them hidden, almost as if our world existed on another plane or dimension of reality.

My senses bathed in the soft touch of pure air, the soothing palette of pale colors and nature's chorus of lulling sounds, highlighted by playful bird songs that filled my heart with wonder and joy.

We stopped in front of a robin's egg blue cottage with roof tiles in all the colors of the rainbow. A wrought iron sign out front read:

Visitors Start Here – Broomsticks Sold Out!

Okay, that was funny. But seriously, I always wished witches could fly.

We signed in at the front desk, got our visitor badges and left Nanya with an excited, gray-haired clairvoyant named Daphne who claimed she had been waiting for us. It was and wasn't a surprise. Clairvoyants were always showing up unscheduled for important moments. This one was a staffer from the Borgo nursery and more than thrilled to take the little fluff into her loving arms.

Faion and I walked to the *Magic Arts Hall* where we were

greeted by Helianna, an impressive looking pyromancer, tall and long-limbed with pronounced cheekbones that helped shape an austere expression.

Pyromancers were fire mages who could twist and convert chemical energy into anything from electricity to explosives to lightning bolts. They could walk through fire and come out unscathed.

Helianna was in her early forties and the Region's second-in-command, answering only to the Great Chanter Horpheus himself, a seasoned mage who excelled at chants, incantations and magic charms and was old enough to remember the first World War in vivid detail.

Helianna wasn't exactly thrilled to see Faion and me, but then again, like most pyromancers, she rarely got excited over anything that wasn't already ablaze with hellish flames or at least being barbecued to some degree.

I was wary of all fire magic and found it hard to conceal the fact. I lowered my head to demonstrate my loyalty and respect for the woman who had dedicated her life to keeping the Deep Down safe.

"I am Luna Mae, here to see my mother, Clara Mae."

She shut the purple leather book in her hands.

"We know who you are," she said.

Clara Mae was a legend in the Deep Down and now I knew why. She had fought against the evils of the world to protect not just a child, but a child that was not even her own flesh and blood.

Helianna's black eyes locked on mine. "Something strange emanates from you," she said, squinting a little as if trying to see through me. "You have changed. Is it that you have found a calling?"

Her dry tone and dead eyes suggested she did not think me capable of having a calling, let alone finding one. Witches with a calling stayed in the Deep Down after all.

A door at the back of the room swung open. Two bulky men entered. Helianna motioned them over. "My guards will escort you to the Infirmary, Luna Mae, Earth witch of Astoria," she said. "I expect you'll have a welcome visit with your mother."

One of the guards stood out. He was young with dark hair and eyes. His gait was easy and assured. He was an electromancer, an electricity wizard who could black out a city the size of San Diego in the blink of an eye.

The other guy was blond and older, probably in his late thirties, and a chronomaster with the ability to briefly halt time—one of the rarest types of mages who were not allowed to leave the Deep Down. The consequences of halting time in the up above could be devastating. No one would take that risk if they could avoid it.

Those two mages were too powerful to be used as escorts. They were of the warrior class. How did their pride even allow such a thing? Did Helianna really view me as dangerous?

As we strolled down the brick path to the Infirmary, things began to make even less sense. Wards pulsed around the charming little houses with the fragrant front gardens like strong, underground currents.

The thing about wards was that they could keep things from entering places, but they could also prevent things from getting out. I wondered which of those objectives these wards served.

Purple sparks ignited underneath my feet, nipping at them as if testing my etheric essence. Magic roiled between the bricks. I had no doubt it would tear through my body and gnaw at my very cells if I made one wrong move.

If I didn't know better, I'd say the Deep Down was preparing for an invasion—bracing itself for war.

It might as well with the Seventh Council already on a warpath.

The Infirmary was a single-story structure with a wide-open floorplan and rows of small, cozy rooms down long, wide hallways.

Once upon a time, mage healers born with the gift of healing filled these corridors, but their numbers had dwindled to a mere handful. The healing was now mostly left to spells and potions and, at times, the conventional medical advancements of the basic world. Unfortunately, nothing had helped Clara Mae.

My heart raced so fast I thought it might burst when we reached my mother's room. The two escorts bowed respectfully before stepping away.

Faion grabbed my hand. "I'll wait for you out here."

His words reached me as if from far away. "Go. Do your things," I told him. "This might be a while."

I took a full breath before pushing through the half open door.

My mother lay on a narrow bed with a turquoise mosquito net canopy and her favorite beige cashmere blanket wrap. Bright sunlight broke through the window, casting playful shadows on her pale face.

My chest ached at the sight of her shut eyes. They had been shut now for so many years. She was unchanged, still the same lovely petite woman in her mid-thirties with delicate features, soft skin and full lips. The evil spell had trapped her mind in a state of perfect stillness, but it also kept her physical existence untouched by time.

It was the cruelest fate and to this day unbreakable by any means known to all the magic dwellers of the Deep Down.

I used my thumb to brush strands of her brown hair away from her forehead, swallowing a sob.

"So much has happened since I last visited," I whispered. I sat down on the wicker armchair next to the bed. "Almost none of it is good."

My throat constricted as I was overcome with the desire that her beautiful eyes would open. I wanted to ask her who was after me, who had put her in this never-ending coma... I knew it had to be the same person and I knew I wanted to kill them.

"I'm so sorry," I said. "Sorry you had to give your life up

for me. I'm not sure it was worth it. I am clueless half the time."

Her eyelids fluttered and for a split second I was sure it was some form of communication, but the fluttering vanished as fast as it began. Every time I went there, my heart broke.

"Did you know?" I wondered out loud. "Who I am? *What* I am?"

I caught myself quickly. With all the wards and security measures in place, I wouldn't be surprised if even this room was monitored.

I stroked Mother's hand, kissed it. I bent down to her ear. "If you can hear me, if these breaths can reach your heart, know this. I will do everything in my power to find the bastards responsible. I will make them pay. And I will find a way to free you from this hell. I promise you this... mother."

I left the room before the tears fell. My dear sweet mother still lay entombed in her own absence, vanished completely yet wholly visible. My words to her were empty, like all the words in all the worlds.

Action was required. What action I knew not, but now I had eternity on my side and there was a way, there had to be a way, to bring her back and to give meaning to my words and this life.

May my vengeance fall hard on any who got in my way.

Chapter 3

FAION AND I LEFT the stone circle behind on our way to the waterfall exit when a familiar voice called my name.

I stopped cold. "Tam," I said, spinning around.

A slim young woman my age stood a few feet away, hands on her hips. She had choppy brown pixie-cut hair and dark, glistening eyes. Tam Nguyen was as bright and beaming as ever, with an engaging smile, impish glint in her eyes and a sunniness in her expression that lit up a room.

She was a year older. I admired not only her endless energy, but the zealous dedication she had shown to the Lunar Order since we were little.

We often trained together over the years. Her talent and laser focus stood out among all the young lunar witches. There weren't many of us left, but Tam exemplified all that was splendid about our kind. By the age of seven, she could control elemental energy with a precision that stunned our teachers. She possessed an eerie ability to block energy before it formed and absorb it as if her own.

Tam had chosen the Deep Down. All witches had to choose between the two worlds when they turned fourteen. Two out of three chose to stay in the Deep Down and train nonstop to become formidable witches.

It had been two years since I last saw Tam, but that felt like an eternity.

Sweat beaded on her forehead. She stood wearing sweats and running shoes back in the stone circle.

"Luna, what the hell?"

"Hey, Tam, oh my god."

Tam grinned. "So, I don't see you last year and now you're trying to sneak out again this year without saying hello."

She pulled me in for a big hug. I had forgotten about her wiry strength.

"Don't crush me," I said, lifting my hands in surrender. "I submit."

"Not my fault," she said. "You *up abovers* are so soft."

She stepped back to study me from head to toe. I was not convinced I met her approval.

"How's your mom, college girl?" she said.

So much had happened, yet I could not burden my childhood friend with any of it—same way I could not burden my best friend in San Diego, Lily. It would be dangerous for anyone to know what I knew, especially a basic.

"Same," I said. "It was good to hold her hand."

Faion nudged me and coughed.

Where are my manners?

"Oh, Faion," I said. "Tam, this is Faion."

Tam arched a brow. "A diviner."

"What? This is some kind of a setup," Faion said, unsure. "Na-uh. No. You can't just guess that. You two talked before. It took me damn near an eon to convince Luna I was a diviner."

I rolled my eyes. "Not many diviners roaming the streets of San Diego."

"It couldn't be more obvious," Tam said. "There's a distorted aura there. You've forgotten your training."

"I was never the diligent witchling you were," I said to Tam.

"That's facts," Faion added. "Home girl's witch game was on life support when we met."

As my two so-called-friends enjoyed mocking me, my eyes caught sight of two small surveillance cameras embedded in the rock above.

Huh. Even the magic realm has turned to tech.

"There's more security than I remember, both tech and spells," I said. "Should we have any cause for concern?"

Tam rolled her lower lip under her upper teeth. After a heavy sigh, she finally said, "Listen, you didn't hear this from me."

"Tam? What?"

"Okay," she said. "Fine. Word is that the troglodytes might be looking to expand their territories."

"Here in the Deep Down?" Faion said.

"According to the sea witches," Tam said.

I chewed on that a long while. "That's just dumb. The troglodytes don't have the numbers or the powers to challenge the Deep Down."

Troglodytes were a warrior faction of reptilian humanoids with scaly skin, long lizard-like tails and uncannily anthropomorphic faces. Instead of hair, a thin bony frill decorated the top of their heads. The cave dwellers were first spotted by other supernatural factions in Northern Italy during the time of the Roman Republic.

Reports of mass troglodyte crossings of the Atlantic went back as far as the late 1600s. They were ceded a few subterranean cave systems on the West Coast where they could mine to their heart's content to mold their armors and weapons. In exchange, they were to keep renegade beasts at bay and away from the Deep Down. They were irritable with notoriously short fuses, quite misanthropic, and mostly stayed out of sight.

Tam's features tightened. "They may have found allies among the necromancers."

"Necromancers?" Faion repeated. "Now that's some nasty magic."

"The nastiest," Tam agreed. "Masters of the dark arts. Their numbers are thought to be dwindling."

"But it still doesn't make sense," I said. "Why would necromancers ever team up with troglodytes? Those factions have no common interests."

Tam started to stretch her legs. "Must have found common interests."

"No offense to the sea witches," Faion said, "but is there independent confirmation of all this?"

"You mean by your people?" Tam said. "Apparently, yes. The strongest diviners and clairvoyants have glimpsed bits and pieces."

"And the master orb?" I queried.

"Clear," Tam said. "The orb's all clear... for now."

"That sounds ominous," Faion said.

"It is," Tam said. "It's very bleeping ominous. Neither of you can share this with anyone in the up above. No one."

"Did she just say *bleeping*?" Faion said out of the side of his mouth.

"You know I heard that?" Tam said.

"He knows," I told her, dismissively. "We're not going to share it, Tam. And we're both grateful you trusted us with this news."

"Well, yeah," she said. "We're friends. You should remember that next time you visit the double D."

"She'll remember," Faion said.

"Did you just divine that?" Tam asked.

"Well, no," Faion said. "I'm just saying, you know, *she'll remember*."

I placed my hand on Tam's shoulder. "Of course, I will."

Tam's eyes filled with tenderness. "Luna, hey, before you go, I know someone who would really like to talk to you."

THE MAGIC-FUELED LIGHT IN the living space was bright enough to make you forget the fact you were deep underground. A woman in her late sixties or early seventies sat low in a cushy, cream-colored armchair. Her eyes were closed—an ancient goatskin-bound book lay in her lap on a folded white apron. A tantalizing pumpkin-spice aroma reached my nostrils.

"Ah, my dear girl, I hoped you would come," the woman said, her eyes still shut, her raspy voice soft and whispery. "First things first. I'm aware of your part in the happenings at Serenity Valley during the metamorphic moon."

If there was a chair behind me, I'd have collapsed back onto it. "I don't even understand..." I began saying, but then her eyes opened and looked right through me.

Memories flooded my brain. I had seen that face before in pictures her grandson had shown me. A wide, honest face with warm brown eyes, thick locks of hair barely turning gray in spots, and a calm smile that welcomed candor and confession from every single person she came across.

Celia Trice. I had no idea Faion had spoken to her.

"I can see you know who I am," she said. "Don't worry

about Faion. Bless his soul, my boy is no snitch. He was not the faithful herald of this news."

She found a cigarette case in an apron pocket and from it retrieved a short cigarette. When she peeled the paper back, all that was left in the end was a pink stick of chewing gum.

I watched, fascinated, as she brought the gum to her lips and licked it. With some delay, I realized she was performing a hypnotizing ritual, a typical spell that diviners used when they wanted to create a distraction.

"Faithful herald?" I said. "Who else of our world was there that night?"

I knew it was likely no one from our world, but I doubted Celia would ever betray her Immortal or morph contact.

Celia bit off a tiny piece of her gum. "One with no name for a name would alter their essence."

Riddles. I suck at riddles.

Celia grinned. "Not to worry, darling, the herald was a benign force."

There was no such thing in all the worlds.

"You wanted to see me?" I said.

She moved forward in her chair and placed the book at her feet. "Why don't you take a seat, sweetheart? Would you like some pie?"

Now she was yanking my chain. I had no time for pie, and she knew it. By now, she must have noticed I was immune to her hypnotizing ritual. "No thanks, Gram's expecting me for dinner."

"Ah, how is Iris? Do give her my regards."

Nice try. "I'll do that. I'm wondering how you knew I was here."

"Your aura. To anyone with my experience in telekinetic etheric fields it is impossible to miss, like a ticking pendulum clock in an empty mansion."

She could hear my aura? That was a new one.

"You sensed... sorry, *heard* my aura from a distance?"

"Like a tidal echo," she said.

That wasn't good. No one wants their aura to run ahead of them, announcing their approach.

"Don't worry your curious mind," she said. "I've had your aura sealed."

I'd have to approach this from a different angle. "And how did you know the aura belonged to me?" I sounded like a broken record.

"Because someone wanted it that way."

"Grandma," I whispered, then plopped down onto the chair like a heavy sack of potatoes.

Celia tilted her head to the side. "She loves you."

Just wait until I get home, Gram. Time to discuss some boundaries.

"She loves me so much that she cast a spell on me, so I'd tick like a time bomb for anyone to hear."

"Only the ears of an old diviner could ever," Celia said. "And there are things that you need to hear."

No shit, Madam Sherlock.

"First, let's both agree to leave Faion out of this. My boy's heart is in the right place, but he's not qualified for this war of giants."

How much did she know? Did she know everything?

"Agreed," I said. "I don't want any harm to come to him."

"Of that we are of one mind," she said.

"He's the best, a true friend. His mother raised him right."

"She did, I'll tell her." Celia blew a bubble that kept growing until it exploded onto her nose and cheeks. "You, too, are a noble soul, Luna Mae."

"I don't know about that."

"You do and I do," Celia said as she picked bubblegum from her face.

What a strangely playful lady.

"I do the best I can," I conceded.

"Lucky for all of us," she added. "Now, young lady, would you like to know of your origins... of the place from which you truly come?"

Was there anything Celia Trice didn't know? Faion might have been right. We should have brought her in from the start.

"Is that a trick question?"

Celia laughed. "No, dear, it's the only question."

"Yes," I said. "Yes, I would."

She filled her lungs, then lay back in her chair and closed her eyes.

I waited. Seconds passed that felt like minutes.

"A very powerful entity gave you to Magistrate Winter," she began. "Someone who walks in danger."

My heart pounded wildly in my chest. "More powerful than a Shadow?"

Celia sighed. "Not many have survived an encounter with a Shadow, and you have seen at least two."

Yeah, I'm a tad bit hard to kill.

In a flash, Celia pulled me to my feet. She placed her hands on my temples. "Why is that?" she said, inhaling before closing her eyes again.

My body stiffened. I fought the urge to swipe her hands away.

Celia eased the pressure on my temples. "It's okay," she said. "I do not wish to see beyond what you want me to see. I'm not an intruder. I searched for signs you might want to confide in me. I found none."

There were none. I wasn't about to let anyone know I was a descendant of the legendary mist riders or that I was, to some degree, immortal. I was still grappling with that revelation myself.

"Please, Celia, tell me everything," I said.

Celia shook her head. "Oh, honey, whoever they are, they won't reveal themselves to me. They're too powerful."

My body felt hollow and cold. I really needed to know.

Celia patted my back. "Are you sure you won't have that pie?"

"I'm good, I knew it was a long shot."

"My dear girl, you must watch your back. Not all fears lead you to the enemy. And not all hopes lead you home."

"I think I understand, but I've seen enemy faces with my own eyes. At least, some of them."

"No, my dear… the enemy is never something you see with eyes. It's something you feel and, when you feel it, your mind will understand, your mind will see. Only then can you choose, Luna."

"I choose me and mine. My Gram, my friends, my life."

"You don't mean that. This is not something I divine, I feel it. The future of our kind may well rest in your hands. There must be choices made."

"Taking sides? War? That sounds like what humanity does and I'm not really interested in repeating their mistakes."

She studied me as if for the first time. "There is no perfect way through this life. This can never be Utopia. This can never be the realization of untarnished virtues. If two very flawed Immortals can kill each other and, in so doing, absorb the other's etheric essence and grow their powers, knock on the door of invincibility, how long until they will lose touch with their patience with lesser beings? Have you ever seen what humans do to harmless insects?"

"Shit, that's really dark."

"Yeah," Celia said. "It is, and you must be the light. You will guide the Shadow who wins your trust. Balance is needed. It may be your instincts, your clarity, your choices… if you are pure, you can be yourself. That is all you need to be."

Okay, but is she really suggesting Chaos as an option? I mean Winter does suck at times, but Chaos? Come on.

Celia's eyes rolled back as her mouth closed in a lopsided manner, the right edge half an inch lower than the left. Her body swayed. I caught her right before she collapsed.

"Don't you fuss," she said as I helped her sit down. "I looked too deep, too long. I may have said too much. That's all for today."

"Do you want Faion?"

"No, this must stay between us. All of it." She reached out to pet my face.

"I understand, Ms. Trice, I do. Thank you."

She sighed. "I am sorry I could not do more, dear soul. And I am sorry for the burden you must carry. I would take it all upon myself if I could."

And now, as I left her, I wavered on my own feet. I wanted to set down this unwanted burden every bit as much as Celia and, I'm sure, my Gram would want to pick it up and carry it far away from me.

Chapter 4

Something was off. I sensed it before I noticed the red circle on my door. Thin threads of energy sparked at the tip of my fingernails as I feared demon animals closing in—the kind that Chaos had sent after me before.

I traced the blood with my right index finger. The stain was the size of a quarter and bright enough to be fresh.

My eyes dropped to the lock—broken. Whoever had left the blood on the door had been inside my apartment or, maybe, were here now.

Calling upon my elemental power, I gently pushed the door open. I stepped through the doorway cautiously, my senses inflamed.

I held my breath as I flipped on the light. The place had been trashed. Tables and chairs toppled, sofa cushions gutted, bookshelves emptied, torn books and papers strewn everywhere. Even my mattress had been cut open.

Good luck finding anything of value in here, evil henchmen.

The kitchen was similarly ransacked. A saucepan was lodged in the window screen over the sink, all the glass having shattered away and collected in both sinks, on the counter and on the floor. The cupboards were damaged, doors bent, missing, punched through. I kicked through a pile of dishes, cups and Tupperware containers to close the refrigerator door.

This was not the work of campus vandals or petty thieves. Nothing had been taken. This was a premeditated search for something not found.

Clutching onto my suitcase, I was very grateful that my personal documents, credit cards, laptop and my favorite outfits were safe inside it.

I suddenly felt very tired. There was so much behind me and so much ahead. My eyes scanned the absurdity of my ravaged belongings and all I could feel was heavy muscle fatigue, the exhaustion from my delayed flight and the whole mess of my insane, disjointed, bizarre existence over the last few months.

A wiser witch would have been on alert or, at least, apprehensive or mildly terrified. I wasn't wise.

I glanced back at the still open front door.

I shouldn't use magic unless completely necessary but screw it.

I spun on my feet and raised my hands to conjure a spell

to fix the lock when a tall man stepped into the doorway.

Electricity shocked my hand as my fusing spell swelled into a shimmering lightning bolt fueled by a million megawatts. Cold sweat oozed onto my neck and face. My heartbeat accelerated to manic and a sudden headache split my skull as I fought to reabsorb the immense energy back into my own life force.

Lunar witches have hyper quick reflexes. It was the only reason I hadn't obliterated Emmet on the spot.

He took a step back, a grave look on his face. "Whoa, I come in peace."

Is peace even an option anymore?

"Sheesh, Emmet. You almost got barbecued."

His lips parted into a sly grin. "Well, it's good to still be here."

"Why are you here?"

"To make sure you're safe," he said. "I stopped by earlier and saw the state of your apartment. I waited a while, then went for coffee. I came back and here you are, ready to roast me alive."

I dropped my head and closed my eyes. Just what I needed, my ex showing up trying to be chivalrous. "How long have you been here?"

"About three hours," he said, eying the phone in his hand. "Three hours and eleven minutes, if we're being precise."

When Emmet and I last spoke, days before I left for Astoria, we agreed we wouldn't see each other again. Well, it was my idea, but he said he'd honor it.

He read my mind. "I swear I wasn't stalking you."

Oy. It was true. I had accused him of stalking more than once and I had mostly been wrong. "I never said that."

"Really, though, I was lured here. Look."

He swiped the screen on his phone and handed it to me.

My eyes glazed over a text that had been sent from my number.

Today 11:14 AM

home tonight

need 2 talk

7pm, my place

Emmet had replied, confirming he'd be there. I should have received his reply since he sent it to my number.

I dug my phone out of my purse and scrolled through my texts. Nothing. The last text received from Emmet was in September, back when we thought there might be something real happening between us.

Before I knew he was a shifter. Before he knew I was a lunar witch.

"My number was spoofed," I said, shocked at the turn of events.

Muscles flexed in his neck. "Doesn't explain why you didn't get my text."

"Who'd want you here to see my place trashed?"

"Not sure that's what they were going for," he said. "Anyway, it was dark. I didn't get a good look at the intruders."

"Wait... you were here when it happened?"

"Caught the tail end. They were finishing up. They came at me, four by my count, fought me a little. Felt like a setup."

"Go back," I said. "Tell me from the start."

"There's not much more. The apartment went dark the moment I pushed the door open, like an unnatural dark. I couldn't see my own hand, so I couldn't make out their faces—if they had faces, they didn't feel human."

Dread pulsed through me. "Shifters?" I said out loud, hoping they weren't morphs on a frenzied path of revenge.

Emmet shook his head. "Beasts of some sort, humanoid, upright fighters but not shapeshifters. I would have smelled it on them."

I pointed at the door. "The blood?"

He shrugged. "Could be mine. Not sure, it happened fast. One second they were on me, the next I was slashing and biting."

It hit me that he had fought off four beasts in an ambush. "Are you okay, Emmet?" I said, reaching for his shoulder.

He grinned. "I play rough and I heal fast."

Is he really trying to flirt right now?

"Is this a victory gloat?"

"Well, they ran off. Either I was doing okay, or they thought I wasn't worth all the trouble."

"I'm sure you were doing okay," I said to reassure his male ego.

"You think?" he said with a glint in his eyes. "Because I

remember you thinking I wasn't worth the trouble."

"That's not getting a response. "Let's stay focused."

"I've patrolled the area," he said. "There's nothing out there."

"I'm just glad you're still in one piece."

He honestly seemed no worse for wear. His black V neck t-shirt clung to his upper body like a glove, his thick brown hair was combed back flawlessly and his jeans... ah, there it was—two long tears ran down the front of his left pant leg while the bottom of the right pant leg had been shredded.

He remained radiant and charming as ever. His warm, hazel eyes, sensual lips and irresistible smile were still—

Snap out of it, Sophie. Stay focused on your own damn self.

"Your shirt..." I stared at his chest, tongue-tied and wanting to die.

"My shirt?" he said. "Ah, right. They ruined the other shirt. I had an extra one in my duffel bag. I came straight from the gym."

"It's just... you don't look like you've been fighting."

"Yeah... I also used some of your hair gel earlier. Hope you don't mind."

"Why would I mind?" I said, trying to avoid the intensity of his eyes.

"I tend to say stupid things around you, Sophie."

I loved hearing my *basic* name on his lips and even as I avoided his eyes, I felt his eyes all over me.

Damn. Way off track. Like big time.

"Emmet, do you think they wanted to hurt you?"

"I don't think so. I showed up early."

"How early?"

"Half an hour." He shook his head. "Actually, closer to forty minutes. Okay, forty-two minutes early. I was impatient and eager to see you."

Stay on track, Sophie.

"And you think they were finishing up?'

"I didn't know at the time," he said, "but after they left, I checked out the apartment. They had pretty much searched everywhere."

"You went through my things?"

Guilt flushed all over his face.

"Never mind," I said. "My flight was late. I would have been here when they were, then you would have arrived shortly after, that is if you had not arrived forty-two minutes early. It stands to reason they wanted us both here at around the same time. The only part I don't understand is why they needed both of us together? There's something we're not seeing."

"There's a lot I'm not seeing," Emmet said. "I don't have clue one, Sophie. All I know is that you're not safe here. We can't guess what's coming next. Maybe we should consider calling the cops."

I paced the floor of my apartment, navigating the debris. I let the facts sink in. Who would do this? Chaos was the obvious suspect, but this seemed like a big step back for him.

I mean, I had pretty much invited him to bring me proof of his claim that the Seventh Council planned to take over the world.

"If paranormal forces are involved, going to the cops is not an option, you know that, Emmet."

"At least come with me. You can spend the night at my place, and we can figure out what to do in the morning."

The dashing doctor wanted to get me alone in his bachelor pad.

Hard pass.

"Not a good idea," I said.

"You can't stay here. The windows are out, the lock is broken."

I shrugged. "I'm hardly helpless."

He looked stumped. "You're not serious about staying here tonight?"

Yeah, my apartment had seen better days, but it was still mine and leaving it behind, even in this state, felt like a betrayal.

"Sophie, I swear, I have no romantic designs," Emmet assured me.

"It's not that," I said. "I wouldn't be able to rest with my place in this order. I want to see what's missing, maybe find a clue."

Also, to deal with the broken items from my past, broken memories, but I did not want to appear vulnerable and encourage him to comfort me.

He was really at a loss for words this time. I could almost hear the gears grinding in his head. "You're going to call *him*?" he said in the end.

Oh, no, Emmet, please let's not go there.

"And by *him*, do you mean Jonas?"

"I don't know his name. I mean the caveman, the old geezer. I bet you think he could protect you."

I was being baited. I wasn't going to bite. "I'm not calling anyone."

"Then I'm staying to help."

I knew there was no shaking his determination. I had to come up with something, or he'd spend the night in my ravaged apartment, watching me slowly lose my mind as I sifted through the wreckage of my life.

"Okay, fine. I'll go to my friend's house. Lily. Her mom's house. I'm spending New Year's Eve there anyway. They'll happily take me in."

He crossed his arms on his chest. "Sounds like a plan," he said, almost defiantly. "And I will escort you there."

"You're a pest, you know that?"

"Call it what you will," he said, "but we both know you won't go otherwise, and I mean to see you to a safe shelter."

"Fine, nineteenth century English dandy, have it your way," I said. "And while you're at it, you can carry my suitcase."

I followed Emmet out. I didn't look back.

Chapter 5

THIRTY MINUTES LATER, I stepped into Lily's open arms. Lucky for me, she was home that night to protect me from the maternal inquisition I would have faced if I'd spent the night alone with Lucia.

"Did you get my text?" I said while she eyed Emmet like a prized calf.

"I just did," she said. "I couldn't believe my eyes. Is everything okay? Am I being punked? You shut down every invite for a sleepover in the past. And why's he here? Are you eloping? Did he get you pregnant? You better not have gotten my friend pregnant, my dude."

I just laughed. She made me laugh. "Nobody's pregnant, Lil."

"Yeah," Emmet said. "I never even got to—"

Lily and I both turned on him with dagger eyes.

"Got to what?" I said.

Emmet went straight red. "Uh," he said.

"*Uh*... My thoughts exactly," I said.

Now Lily laughed. "I take it this is Emmet."

"Yep," he said, reaching out his hand. "I'm Emmet."

They shook. "I'm Lily. Charmed." She stepped aside to let us enter.

"It's been a long night," I said.

"What the hell happened?" Lily said as she locked the door.

"Nothing," I said. "Campus thieves broke into my place. Emmet chased them away before they could take anything."

"Oh, my poor dove, that's hardly *nothing*," Lucia said, walking out from the kitchen wearing a red apron and yellow latex gloves. She took off the gloves one after the other and wiped both hands on her apron. She hugged me tight, then gently brushed back my hair. "Are you okay? All in one piece?"

"I'm fine."

"That's Emmet," Lily said. "Don't worry, he hasn't gotten her pregnant."

"I should hope not," Lucia said. "What a thing to say. Not everything is an opportunity for your mordant jokes, sweetheart."

"It's all good, Lucia," I said. "I'm just grateful to you both."

Lucia smiled and took my hand. Her dark hair was pulled

up into a ponytail, her bronze hoop earrings jangling as she turned to Emmet.

"I was going to make up the sunroom for you, Sophie, but since you brought your *boyfriend*, you two can have my room."

In her mid-forties, Lucia didn't look a day older than thirty.

Emmet's eyes widened as he gave Lucia a toothy grin. Literally every young man who had ever met Lucia formed an instant *Mrs. Robinson* crush.

"The sunroom will be fine," I said. "Emmet was just leaving."

"I just wanted to make sure she got here in one piece," he added.

"At the very least that has earned you a warm meal," Lucia asserted.

In light of past misfortunes, I would have preferred Lucia not break bread with any more supernatural beings like Emmet. It still made me cringe to imagine her both in bed with Chaos and doing his evil bidding. It did not help that she neither consented nor could remember any of it. I could. In fact, it was burnt forever in my memory.

"Isn't it a bit late for dinner?" I said, knowing it would do no good.

Lucia grinned. "In my world it's never too late for dinner."

Lily mouthed a *no kidding* behind Lucia's back to confirm the veracity of what her mother had said.

In the living room, colorful pieces of patterned paper lay scattered all over the couch and carpet. Lucia stacked them on the coffee table as she talked.

"It's so good to see you, Sophie," she said while she and Lily picked up the last of the scrap paper. "I did hope you'd spend more time in Astoria with your grandma. Is she doing well?"

"Boundaries, Mom," Lily said.

"Gram's great. Astoria was quiet, cold and snowed in," I said.

"Sounds wonderful," Lucia said before disappearing to the kitchen.

On the bookshelves, paper animals, paper flowers, and even a paper dragon stood in a row. Apparently, Lucia had taken up origami.

Lucia returned suddenly with a platter full of bright colored macarons and petit fours. "I wouldn't mind a bit of weather," she said, considering Emmet. "Your boyfriend is more than welcome to stay the night. It's obvious how much he has missed you."

"Emmet and I are just friends."

Lucia nodded. "Well, good friends are precious."

"Mom..." Lily said.

I popped a pink macaron into my mouth and chewed slowly. The almond paste pastry melted on my tongue. I licked my lips. I might as well take control of this conversation.

"Emmet stopped by my place," I said. "He noticed the open door and ended up physically confronting the vandals."

"Oh my god," Lily said, covering her mouth. "Were you home?"

"I was on a plane," I said. "Emmet played the hero."

"I should say he did," Lucia said. "What did the police say?"

The police. Right. That's what basic people would have done, call the police. My complete mental and physical fatigue made it impossible for me to come up with a plausible lie.

Smooth Emmet came to my rescue. "They're looking into it."

Lucia nodded, unconvinced. I could see questions forming.

"Anyway, the door lock was unfixable. Emmet insisted I not stay in my apartment in that condition, so here I am."

"Good man, Emmet," Lucia said. "Our Sophie can be stubborn."

Lily's face lit up. "Can be? Huh. No. Sophie is next level, *has-to-be* stubborn. Like brick-wall stubborn, bullfight stubborn, dude, I mean Sasha Fierce stubborn, Buddha at the lotus tree—"

"We get it," I said, stopping her.

"Do you have renter's insurance?" Lucia said.

Did I?

"It was nice meeting you. I appreciate the invite, but I really do have to get going," Emmet said. "Sophie, may I have a word?"

"Another time," Lucia said. "Safe travels."

"Later, dude," Lily said.

I followed Emmet out. His features sharpened as we shut the door behind us and stood on the front steps.

"I know I don't need to tell you this," Emmet said, "but the less they know the better. It's not a matter of trust. They seem nice enough."

"If you knew you didn't need to tell me, then why did you?"

He stared down at me, his eyes sparking with golden specks. "Why do you do that? Push everyone away."

His sincerity unnerved me. A night breeze chased playfully through the violet leaves of a blue Jacaranda tree across the street.

"It's the best way to get some space," I said, quieter than planned. "I obviously won't tell Lily or her mom anything about anything."

He scratched the back side of his shoulder. "Listen, I can stay out here in the shadows, stand guard on the house."

Wolf shifters and their everlasting need to be the alpha.

"Concentrate on your own safety, Emmet. They know how to find you and they have no qualms about hurting you. Believe me."

"I can take care of myself. If they come, I won't run."

Another fool who would die to prove a point.

"Okay, I know you're a badass, just please don't go home tonight. Go somewhere else, a friend... the pack. How does that work, are you registered with the local pack? Is there even a pack in San Diego?"

He grinned. "You don't know much about shifters, do you? Didn't they teach you all this down in the big below?"

"It's the Deep Down," I said.

"I know," he said. "I listened when my elders taught me about all the supernatural beings. I'll refresh your memory. A shifter will not move to a new habitat unless there is an established pack in place. Whether we register as a permanent member or not, we still have a bonding ceremony where we take the oath of allegiance."

"So, go to them tonight," I insisted. "Let them protect you."

He sighed. "You're as stubborn as Lily says. It's the last thing I want to do, but if it puts your mind at ease, I'll check into the local den."

I nodded. "Thank you."

"I'll call you in the morning. And, Sophie, you should reconsider calling the cops. It might not be a bad idea."

"What can the basic cops do?" I said.

"They won't find prints or clues, but they might keep the intruders away for a day or two. Most cops have body cameras now. Supernatural thugs hate cameras even more than they hate cops."

"Sure, I'll give it some thought. Now, please go find the pack."

He leaned in to kiss my cheek. His breath smelled minty and inviting.

"I missed that," he said.

"Just be safe tonight," I said, trying not to shudder.

Emmet Groshek was one of the good guys, steadfast and strong, but not immortal. His courage only made him more vulnerable, and all I wanted was that he should stay forever in one piece.

I closed the door between us and pressed my head against it. Emmet thought I'd be safe in a basic home, but the truth was that my being here would only invite trouble onto my friends' heads.

Chaos had already recruited Lucia once. To him there were no rules to the game. He made the rules and then forgot them. There was no shortage of destructive bastards in any world—magic, basic or otherwise. The only difference was that Chaos and his dark Immortal army could destroy every-single-thing all the way down to a cellular level.

On second thought, I was the best defense my friends could have, and I would sleep better that night knowing they were close.

Chapter 6

THIN STREAKS OF BLOOD rolled down the wood, drenching the welcome mat. It was as if an open wound oozed from the center of the door. Thank god I listened to Emmet and didn't stay at my apartment last night.

I lay awake until just before dawn, staring at the sky through the glass walls of Lucia's sunroom. I listened to the sounds of the night outside, recreating the dark street in my mind's eye.

When the sun broke, I sneaked out, hoping that daylight would be enough to shield my friends from malevolent beings.

The bloody gash on my door was noticeable from the bottom of the stairs. Hurrying to the door, I quickly curled my hands into fists, beckoning my elemental power. Energy swelled and sizzled on my palms, then detonated, sparking and howling as it began to envelop the blood.

I did not care if the reverberations reached other super-natural creatures or the orbs or even the Deep Down itself. I did not care if any of my neighbors were awake and watching magic spill from my hands. All I cared about was that my invocation mustered enough might to crush and conquer the blood-preserving spell on my door in the most conspicuous manner possible.

I shut my eyes, overwhelmed by my own gathering force as it collided with the foreign power. The door jerked and rattled on its hinges. Black smoke emanated from the red liquid as I drew the spell out bit by bit.

My magic began to assert itself inside the blood. A sharp ache cut through me, forcing me to bend over. Some powerful entity was trying to intercept my spell. I clenched my teeth and pushed harder against the resistance, bringing the full weight of my power upon the blood sorcery.

Yeah, that's right, I'm here, come and get me.

The smell of boiling blood invaded my nostrils as a hissing sound pierced my ears. I grunted. I shook. I persisted. The blood began to retreat, shrinking slowly down to a final fizzy bubble until it burst and every drop was gone.

My head throbbed.

Now my enemies knew I was back at the apartment. They knew I had kicked their sorcery's ass, their spell just collapsing under my strength.

They felt that. Oh, yes, they did.

I covered myself with a glowing energy shield. I was taking no chances. There would be no pitch-black surprises for me.

Sorry, assholes.

Pushing the door open, I stepped through the mess. I surveyed the debris. No signs of any additional damage. Everything looked the same except the coffee table. It was now, somehow, standing on its four legs.

I walked to it slowly, still safe inside my shield. There was a folded paper on the table. I nudged the paper and watched as it unfolded like it had been waiting for me to arrive.

The note was written in blood.

To save the crossbreed
The witch must succumb
To the Lord of soul swallowers

I rubbed the nape of my neck. What did that mean? Assuming the witch was me, who was the crossbreed that needed saving and, more importantly, what exactly were the soul swallowers? They didn't sound fun.

My trail of thought was interrupted by a gentle knock on the door. *What do you know?* The soul swallowers were polite fiends.

I marched to the door and yanked it open. A gray-haired man in a dark blue suit stared at me. He looked like Emmet if he had grown thirty years older in a single night and had an old scar just above his right eyebrow.

For a moment, I was unable to speak, then I remembered I had seen the man before, at a distance, standing next to Emmet at the mall. His father.

"My name is Ken Groshek," the man said. "I'm sorry for the intrusion."

That word held a different meaning for him, no doubt, than it did for me.

I stepped outside and closed the door. I was not in the mood for a conversation about the sorry state of my place.

"How may I help you?" I said.

His eyes focused on the door behind me. "Could we talk inside?"

I shook my head. "We can't. Sorry."

This didn't seem to faze him. He breathed out through his nose and locked his eyes on mine. "It might be a shot in the dark, but you might be the only person who can assist me."

"Assist you? I don't understand."

"Emmet's missing," Ken Groshek said. "He thinks the world of you, Miss Collinsworth. He said you know what he is. Is there any chance you have heard from him?"

His voice broke on the last syllable. His breathing became labored as he adjusted the cuffs of his linen jacket.

"Emmet's fine, Mr. Groshek," I said, plastering a grin of reassurance on my face. "He's with the local pack."

He shook his head. "Emmet was taken last night outside the pack compound. A perimeter Delta glimpsed the abduction, but he failed to intervene."

The elements stilled. My heartbeat raced. I wanted to believe I had heard him wrong, but the sad certainty in Mr. Groshek's eyes overwhelmed me.

I relented and opened the door so we could talk inside. His jaw went slack as he absorbed the frantic disarray of my studio apartment.

"Tell me everything you know," I said.

"Five men in hoods attacked Emmet," he explained. Thankfully, he chose not to inquire further about my gutted apartment. "The Delta guard howled for backup, then left the overlook immediately to help, but by the time he and the others could get down there, a black van with no plates was racing off."

"Who relayed the story to you?"

"The pack's leader. He called me from Emmet's phone. He must have dropped it during the fight."

Knowing Emmet, the dropping of his phone was intentional. "Where's the phone now?"

"Two wolf shifters brought it to me. His last text was to you. I thought maybe you knew what he meant."

"Can I see it?"

He furrowed his brow. "Haven't you read it yet?"

Even though I knew the text wouldn't be there, I checked my phone anyway. Nothing.

Stupid, stupid phone.

"The message never got through," I said.

With a sigh, Mr. Groshek handed me his son's phone.

> *They're here. U not safe. Go home.*

Home? He didn't mean the apartment. He meant the Deep Down. Did his father guess that? Did he even know I was a witch? He certainly knew he could mention shifters to me.

"I was hoping you could explain his shorthand," Mr. Groshek said. "It sounds as if both of you might know the kidnappers."

I shook my head. "I don't. I imagine Emmet assumed they're the same guys who wrecked my apartment, but I wasn't here to see them."

He nodded slowly several times, then rubbed his forehead. "I'm probably way off and I mean no offense, but I have to ask. Are you a shapeshifter, Miss Collinsworth?"

The question surprised me. I stifled an involuntary laugh. "No, Mr. Groshek, I most certainly am not. And please, call me Sophie."

He looked down and sighed. "Maybe you can't help then." He flashed his worried eyes. "Or maybe you know about this."

The troubled man handed me a folded paper. It looked identical to the one I found on my coffee table, but the note was written in black marker ink, not blood.

> *Find the witch. Only she can save the crossbreed.*

Okay, so the cat was out of the bag. Ken Groshek had very clearly been clued in about who I was, but somehow remained uncertain about me. He suspected I was the witch and now I suspected Emmet was the crossbreed—half basic, half shapeshifter.

"Where did you find this?" I asked, glancing to the note as if all the answers I would ever need were contained there.

"Nailed to Emmet's door."

Two weeks from starting my new life abroad, and here I was, being thrown back into the middle of hell with no direction home. This was my destiny, to be dragged back again and again to a role I did not select but was born to play. I used to think destiny was a good thing, but it is merely something that is unavoidable.

I might as well accept it and dive in headfirst.

"I can't share details," I said, "but I promise you I'll do everything possible to get Emmet back unharmed."

Mr. Groshek bowed his head. He seemed deeply touched, absorbing my words as if they were a needed elixir. "I'll take you at your word. Be careful, Sophie. My son is no average shifter. Only a thing of great power could have taken him."

I have some ideas.

"The pack has agreed not to inform his mother yet," he went on. "I thought it would only serve to devastate her. The woman would fly out here from Rhode Island and put her own life at risk to save him."

Emmet's mother was a shapeshifter. Shifters lack control

when a family member is in peril. She wouldn't leave a stone unturned and in so doing, she'd jeopardize not only her life, but also Emmet's.

"You made the right call," I said. "Let's not complicate this further."

Ken Groshek grimaced, overcome by the agony of letting go. "My son trusts you. I must choose to do the same."

A sinking feeling hit my stomach as I shut the door. The world started spinning, as if my equilibrium was off. Everything was happening too fast.

Mist rider or not, I was still vulnerable, still outplayed. I was fighting against forces with thousands of years more experience than me.

This had Chaos's footprint all over it. He had a habit of sending messages via monsters and he liked to get my attention by hurting people close to me.

It was all my fault. I had basically handed him Emmet's head on a platter when I mentioned Emmet's name to him outside the hospital.

A possible silver lining was that Chaos knew better than to hurt Emmet. If his intention was to get my attention, he had succeeded.

I intended to break every treacherous bone in his body and chew his guts out when I got my hands on him. I'd had it with his sick games. The problem was I had no idea how to smoke Chaos out from whatever deathly backwater he currently called home. Maybe there was still some connection to

Chaos in Lucia's subconscious mind, a way to contact him through her.

No. That was my rage speaking for me. I would not put Lucia and Lily at risk, even for this. Winter had loved pointing out that my emotional response to conflict was my biggest flaw.

The only thing I could think to do was get the police involved like Emmet had urged. I'd tell them I had a stalker. I'd tell them he had gone apeshit in my apartment, and that I was worried he might target my friends next as they had provided me shelter and safe harbor. Hopefully, they'd keep a watchful eye on them while I tried to hand the Lord of soul suckers his balls.

The bastard had his hostage. He had as much leverage as he would ever need over me. Lily and Lucia were probably in no immediate danger, but I wouldn't overlook any dreadful possibility.

More instructions in the form of riddles would likely follow, but one way or the other I'd get to the bottom of this, with or without cryptic clues.

Faion. *Shit.* I wanted to leave him out, too, but shit. I needed him. Despite Celia's plea and despite my own reservations, what choice did I have? As far as detecting unknown etheric fields and tracing residual magic I was beyond useless and Faion was all the rage.

I glanced at my phone on the coffee table. I should have ditched that thing as soon as Emmet mentioned the fake text. I hurled a small spark of electricity at the screen. The spark sizzled as it invaded the inside mechanisms and made my smart phone dumb. A small implosion shook the coffee table as the phone started to smoke like a miniature industrial chimney.

On my way to the police station, I dumped what was left of my cursed phone into a trash bin marked for *Pet Waste Only*.

Chapter 7

A DAY LATER, AFTER the police had combed the apartment, Faion and I walked through my door. I'd called him in Astoria from the police station the day before and briefed him on our way from the airport.

He crossed his arms on his chest and scanned the apartment. "Damn, you weren't joking when you called this a dumpster fire. Place looks like five crackheads forgot where they'd hid their stash."

I bent my face at him, trying and failing not to smile. "Why would you think I was joking?"

"Females blow shit out of proportion."

Females? Give me patience.

He was lucky I needed him, or I would have put him on blast. "Dude, really? What do you think?"

He shrugged. "This a day-after-a-frat-party, feng shui

apocalypse. I'm not even mad. They fucked up yo' crib with that hurricane flavor, like FEMA needs to be cc'd on this."

I tapped my feet on the floor. "Are you done?"

"Like a bull in a vagina shop."

Oh, for crying out loud.

"You're hardly the expert on that," I said. "How about we nudge this conversation back to reality? Do you think the soul swallowers did this?"

That shut him up, finally. He stared at me with wide open eyes, then started for the door. "Oh, hell no. I don't even know what that is, but I damn sure want to keep it that way. Uh-uh. Nope. My ass is leaving the building. I'm black Elvis. Show's over."

My hand twitched. The door immediately slammed so he couldn't leave.

Faion stopped cold. He closed his eyes, breathing intensely. "If I stay for a minute, just to listen, then you need to promise not to use your scary-ass *Carrie* magic. I don't want any pig's blood poured on me."

I waited until he turned around and then hit him with pleading eyes. "I'm sorry about the door. Sometimes that kind of happens involuntarily."

"Mm-hmm, that's what Carrie would say," he said. "And I do not want to be the black dude who dies at the start of a horror movie. Or the middle. Or the end. I want out of the whole Stephen King multiverse. Feel me?"

"It's just been a lot, Faion," I said with a heavy exhale.

"You're the best guy. You know that I think that. In fact, I think you're simply divine."

"That's better," he said.

I flashed him my biggest smile. "Maybe you might, maybe, possibly consider using that big, powerful divining power of yours? You know, for a loyal friend in need."

"Don't overcook it. I'm not hetero," he reminded me. "I don't respond to some of that coquettish manipulation, but I do respect it."

"So, you'll help? Just a teensy-weensy?"

He rolled his eyes. "You need to shield any reverberations. I know that's a lunar witch thing, sealing magic scenes."

"Yeah, sure, I'll do my best," I told him, "but every minute that passes could prove crucial for Emmet's chances of survival. I pulled him into this. I have to get him out."

"Is the scene undisturbed?"

"Think so, for the most part," I said. "I left things as they were."

He readied himself. "Gran warned me not to use my powers above ground. Not again. I agreed. This is not cool, lying to my gran."

Ah, that explained it. Celia had gotten to him already. As much as I hated that both of us were breaking promises to her, I couldn't come up with any other way to search for Emmet.

I put my hand on his shoulder. "I won't forget this, Faion."

"I won't let you."

Sealing another's magic wouldn't be easy. I'd finally learned to do an adequate job with my own magic in enclosed spaces, but executing that same trick for a friend was far more challenging. Winter or Chaos could do these things as easily as breathing. They were ancients and they were shadows. I was twenty-two.

I flung my hand on top of Faion's head. Underneath my fingertips, his pulse quickened as his blood rushed to the crown of his skull where the magic in my own blood was summoning it. Our auras connected as they flared above us, Faion's a lemon yellow and mine olive green.

A pale pink light flickered around us, then expanded in traversing lines snaking about the room, surrounding the door and windows. No magic reverberations would escape the walls of the apartment.

"Done," I said, breathless. "The room is sealed."

Faion paced about the space, artfully avoiding discarded objects on the floor. "First, I'll need to hold something of yours," he said. "Something quite personal, so I can eliminate your own etheric essence. That *tough witch* vibe must be all over the place."

I headed for the closet and found the San Diego Chargers shirt I had slept in the night before my trip to Astoria. It was at the top of my hamper. The entire closet had been untouched. Strange.

Faion moved to the center of the room and held the shirt

to his heart. "I'll need to touch things they've touched, connect to any fleeting residue."

"Uh, the police dusted for fingerprints," I confessed. "Could that—"

"—be a problem?" he said, sternly. "Yeah. That wasn't smart."

"Maybe not."

"For sure not," he said. "Wait, did you say there was a blood note?"

Of course, why didn't I think of that?

I tiptoed through broken glass and stepped over English muffins to grab my purse. I rummaged through the contents and pulled out the note.

Faion held his breath. "This is foul," he said, unfolding the piece of paper. "They used actual blood to write this."

"That's why it's a blood note."

"The soul munchers don't play," he said. "I'm not sure I can intuit creatures I didn't know exist and don't know how they look."

"Only one way to find out."

He shook his head, then squatted and closed his eyes. He clutched the note in his right fist and began to chant under his breath. I held my own breath as his lips quivered and his aura became a sharp, vibrant gold that circled him quickly before being sucked into the fibers of the paper note, leaving tiny golden tendrils floating in the air.

Faion's eyes darted about under his closed eyelids.

"The scents are familiar," he said.

My heart surged in my chest. "What are they?"

"At least one Immortal slinked through these walls."

"Chaos," I said. "What a complete bastard."

"There's more. These are hard scents to distinguish."

Right. The minions, the soul suckers, the asshats that abducted Emmet.

"Scaly beings, cross species, armored, warlike. They stand on two legs, I think, they're reptile-like but humanoid. Four foul beasts."

It can't be. Those rumors were true.

"Troglodytes. You mean troglodytes?"

Faion's eyes snapped open. "Yeah, I guess, whatever. They are foul, the very foulest souls. Rotting. Their blood is rancid. Old blood. Almost like the dead... and I got a whiff of *wolfie* in here, too. Your shifter."

"Emmet," I said. "Yeah, he was in here."

"I'm thoroughly creeped out by what I just felt," Faion added.

"Me, too. Troglodytes never step out into the basic world, not since the beginning of time. They have stayed hidden from the human realm. They have a strong disgust for weak, disease-ridden creatures, humans especially, and I don't think their blood is supposed to be rancid."

Tam had mentioned that the troglodytes were teaming up with necromancers. Could that have something to do with it? What an odd coupling. Necromancers were equally lethal, but they always stuck with their own agenda. They did not want souls to swallow, they wanted souls to command.

What possible common goal could these factions hold?

I rubbed my temples. This was far above my paygrade. How was I supposed to fight not only against Chaos and the troglodytes, but also necromancers who could blow life back into the dead and then command the resurrected like a zombie army? Only the Eternals had been keeping the necromancers in check.

Had Chaos conned both the eaters of living souls and those who ruled dead souls to join his rebellion? If so, we were all screwed.

Faion tapped the piece of paper in his hand. "This isn't a Sophie and Faion adventure. We go to college, we share memes and text each other emojis," he said, reading my mind. "We can't deal with this alone. We need help."

"I agree one hundred, but who are you thinking about? The Deep Down? Are they really going to risk open war with the Immortals just to come to the aid of a single shapeshifter?"

Shapeshifters were not even allowed in the underground realms. They had no affiliations, no loyalties at all with the beings of the Deep Down. Anything they might learn or steal, it was feared would likely be used to advance their primitive, violent, clan-driven natures.

Faion's face turned cold. "Don't play dumb, honor roll

girl. I can see you're lying even to yourself. You know who we going to call. That Methuselah motherfucker. That rickety old hunk-slash-stalker who probably slept with Cleopatra *and* her mother. Your icy hot grinch. Mr. Mean."

I shook my head. "There must be another way."

"Dude owes you. Not only did you save their collective asses, you saved his own personal immortal ass. It's time to collect."

That bridge has been burned to ash.

Faion sighed. "Do you want to save your boy toy or not?"

For the first time Faion was not nice, but he did have a point. "I don't even know if we can find Winter or contact him. We didn't end on good terms."

"I don't need to hear all that," Faion said. "Whatever happened, I already know it was his fault, whether you believe it or not. It was."

Everything in me screamed not to do this but... priorities. I'd deal with my emotional misgivings and betrayed principles on my own time.

"Okay, Faion, give me your phone."

"What happened to your phone?"

"Gone. It had been compromised."

He reluctantly handed me his phone. "Don't compromise this one."

"I won't," I said and started typing.

Faion raised an eyebrow. "You just going to text an Immortal? They got smart phones now? Okay. What's next?

Necromancers going to be swiping right on my Tinder pho-to? Troglodytes going to challenge me to an epic game of *Words with Friends*?"

I kept typing, ignoring him.

Urgent! Contact me at this number.

"You memorized his number?" Faion said with a raised eyebrow.

"You have a Tinder account?" I snapped back.

Faion's phone rang, startling me.

A Drake song, big bass, fuzzy synths.

"You see?" Faion said with a grin. "He thirsty, two second callback."

I glared at him and answered the phone.

"*It's I*," Winter said. "*What do you need?*"

He sounded chill and casual in a pre-Tudor sort of way, as if our relationship hadn't disintegrated into little more than hostile barbs and threats, both veiled and unveiled, before we parted ways.

"My place has been sacked," I said. "Like totally tossed and trashed. Faion sensed an Immortal and maybe four troglodytes."

Silence. I tapped my fingernails on the screen.

"*When did this occur?*"

"Two days ago."

"*Your home was invaded two days ago and you're telling me now?*"

He sounded pissed. Good.

"Yes. Isn't that what I just said?"

I'd have preferred never telling you, genius.

More silence, followed by a heavy exhale. "*Fucking child.*"

I lowered the phone to my waist to avoid unleashing a stream of pointed profanity. When I regained control, I returned the phone to my ear.

"There's more," I said. "Emmet... you know, the wolf."

"*I know who he is,*" Winter said.

"They lured him to me, took him, then left a message in his blood."

Too much, too soon? This news might even please him. Instead of helping me, he might track down those responsible to give them high fives.

"*You are a sharp pain in my ass,*" he said. "*Be there in one hour.*"

Chapter 8

WINTER KNOCKED ON THE half open door. My lungs stopped cold. I hadn't realized how seeing him would affect my breathing or turn my skin instantly clammy. He stood there in the flesh—tall and blond with perfect posture, high cheekbones and those deep-blue eyes. He was both lean and muscular, and his bearing had the alert, contained violence of predator cats.

He entered rooms as if he owned them, even while wearing the garb of a suburban dad—a brown polo shirt and khakis. He locked his simmering eyes on mine with purpose.

His confidence and the irrational fear he always made me feel pissed me off.

Winter surveyed the damage, flaring his nostrils as if he could sniff out the truth.

No one wants their nemesis to be attractive. His dimples

and his full lips always ruined my train of thought.

Thankfully, Faion cleared his throat.

Winter looked at him for the first time. "Mr. Trice."

That just about did it. I lost the little patience I had left. "Oh, for fuck's sake, his name is Faion."

We were past all that crap. I wanted to make that very clear.

Winter furrowed his brow. "What trouble have you found this time?"

I had to admit, he was uniquely gifted at triggering me.

"This time? When did I ever find trouble? *You* found me, remember? *You* got me involved in a war I didn't know existed. *You* exposed me to the most deviant, monomaniacal dickwad in the universe as part of *your* own personal, bullshit rivalry. And then there's the time *you* tricked me into initiating the slaughter of thousands of shifters."

"Morphs," he corrected me. "Bloodthirsty metamorphic shifters."

"I know. I was there, remember? Because of *you*."

"Actually, no, not those times. My inference referred to other times. For instance, the time *you* were about to physically couple with a shapeshifter who easily fed *you* lies and now here *you* are again, feeding on more lies, or at least freshly baked delusions despite all warnings."

"What about the time *you* followed me to the airport and—?"

"Hello," Faion cut in.

"What?" we both said, glaring at him.

Faion shrugged. "Hey, I wanted to bring you back to the task at hand, but it's obvious you two have some... unresolved issues. I'll be outside... on planet Earth. Call me when you're done with whatever this is."

Winter chuckled after Faion left. "Your friend must have noticed your schoolgirl crush on me. It made him uncomfortable."

"You have that ass backwards, genius. He thinks *you're* all about my business because you jumped at the opportunity to help me."

His expression switched to somber. "I responded because when you're involved, the stakes are too high to avoid your sour disposition."

"Likewise, I would have loved to avoid your failed personality."

Something behind me caught his eye. I turned and saw nothing beyond the complete disarray of my apartment.

"Is the ward yours?" he said.

Ward? "I don't put up wards willy-nilly," I said. "I used some crisscrossing energy beams to seal reverberations. Is that what you mean?"

He ignored me and stepped closer to the wall. Now I saw it. A thin, red energy flickered as it tried to contain itself.

"I have no idea what that is," I said.

"Whatever it is, your shielding beams are irritating the hell out of it."

Winter lunged at me, grabbing my shoulders to pull me

against him as we spun away. His much larger body covered mine from head to toe.

The wall exploded behind his back. My ears rang as I turned in a daze. Plaster and wood pelted Winter's back like a machine gun. Blood poured out of his neck, but he kept steady hold of me, shielding me from a second blast.

Sharp shards zipped past us and planted in the opposite wall. Two shards had planted in his shoulder and I knew more had pierced his back and legs.

I fought with all my strength to break free from Winter's embrace, but I was easily outmuscled. He let go suddenly, and I stumbled backwards. There was blood on my arms and shoes. Winter's blood.

The wall where the ward had lingered had been obliterated down to shreds of wooden support beams. The opposite wall had taken heavy damage from projectile wall debris puncturing gaping holes everywhere.

As if the damage wasn't enough already.

"You didn't need to do that," I said, patting dust off my clothes and hair.

"It's an instinct," he said. "Like when your wolf howls at the moon."

Why did he make it so hard to like him?

I bit my lip. "Well, are you okay? There are shards of everything sticking out of your arms and a few more in your back."

Instinctively, I waved my hand and all the shards fell

out of his body.

"And you didn't need to do that," he said, raising an eyebrow, "but thank you."

"I trust the wounds will still heal on their own?"

"Already healing."

"Of course, they are," I said. "And thank you or your instinct, whichever was responsible for the gallantry."

"Not necessary," he said.

Faion walked in with caution. The blood and mayhem he witnessed stopped him in his tracks.

It's not a party until someone spills blood.

"The blood's not mine," I said. "A sneaky ward exploded."

Faion nodded a few times. "How did I not hear a thing?"

Ah-huh, my sealing spell had worked. No magic echoes would leave these walls.

"Don't be so proud of yourself," Winter said. "It's just a sealing spell."

Damn, I must have been smiling.

He grabbed the collar of his bloodied shirt and pulled it over his head.

Faion was immediately mesmerized. Winter's golden tattoo of a regal double-headed eagle shone on his carved chest like amber.

He walked to the kitchen and bent over the sink. His entire back and his bulging triceps were covered in an angry red—his minced flesh was raw and still bleeding as if he had just been skinned alive.

Faion and I watched as his flesh quickly regenerated. Winter's body created new cells and collagen to heal the lacerations briefly before the new scar tissue slid off his body as fast as it had formed. What was left were dozens of pink markings on healed skin. Seconds after it appeared, the pink faded and the flesh below became identical to his undamaged skin.

Almost as amazing, he was able to wipe off his entire back with wet paper towels by contorting his shoulders and powerful arms.

I reached over to close Faion's mouth which was hanging open.

"Let me guess," I said to Winter. "You have a spare shirt in the old Civic."

"You remember one of my lessons."

"Yeah, be prepared," I said. "Am I a boy scout now?"

"I think you also have to pee standing up," Faion quipped.

"Diviner, our witch tells me you sensed an Immortal's essence," Winter said, ignoring Faion's ill-timed joke. "Describe it."

Faion cleared his throat. "Yeah, it was, um, a pungent scent. No offense."

"I cannot be offended," Winter said. "And I, too, can smell it."

"I mean, it has to be Chaos, right?" I said.

"It does not have to be anything," Winter said. "The shadow part of Chaos does not register. This could have been one of his immortal underlings or some other unknown player.

Any assumption must be proved."

"Yeah, obviously," I said.

Winter brushed his hair back with his fingers. "Let me see that blood note and tell me exactly what happened, beat by beat. Leave nothing out."

I complied. He listened with intense interest and zero interruptions. I told the story slowly with extensive details, all the way down to the way Ken Groshek was dressed when he knocked on my door.

"And do you have that note?" Winter asked when I was done. "The one left for the wolf's father?"

How had that not crossed my mind? "No, I'm sorry. I didn't think."

"Would it be possible for you to retrieve it?"

And, of course, I did not ask Ken Groshek for a phone number. He did have Emmet's phone, but that number was stored in the phone I threw out, and I hadn't memorized it.

Sure, there was a good chance Ken Groshek stayed at Emmet's place, but I somehow had no idea where Emmet lived. Brilliant, just brilliant. For all my so-called drama with Emmet, I barely knew the first thing about him.

"I guess we could try the hospital where Emmet works. They might be able to give us information of Ken's whereabouts or Emmet's apartment."

"Which hospital?" Winter asked.

"Sharp Memorial."

"Leave that to me," he said. "I'll acquire the information."

His expression warned me not to ask how, which was great, because I had no desire to learn of his methods.

"Great," I said.

"So, that's all of it?" Winter said.

"That's it, the whole shebang... wait, there was one odd thing, maybe, I don't know. They left my closet completely intact."

Why did I say that? My clothes went flying across the room as Winter rummaged through my tanks, jumpers, camisoles, tube tops, club jeans, the skirts I no longer wore, and boots I'd grown sick of.

"There's nothing of value here," he concluded.

"As far as magic? I could have told you that," I said, irritated.

"As far as anything," he said under his breath.

I might have erupted at that, but I was mortified at the sight of my Wonder Woman panties that had ended up hanging from the blue, stained glass light fixture.

I dated a guy sophomore year with a superhero fetish. Sue me.

Winter rubbed his chin. "Something gave them pause."

"Probably them panties," Faion said.

Winter worked something out in his head. "They opened the closet door and they sensed you, all of you, for the first time."

My essence. Oh god, they knew I was something more than a witch.

"They didn't know they were in a witch's den?" Faion asked.

Winter's eyes fell on mine. I gave him a knowing glare.

"I don't know what they knew," Winter said.

Crisis averted. The less Faion knew about me, the safer for him.

Winter picked up his shredded shirt and squeezed it into a ball. Sizzling orange flames formed in and around his fist. His magic always shook me. Immortals weren't supposed to possess elemental magic, but he was more than Immortal—he was a shadow warrior. I had no idea what they were truly capable of, and it would be better never to find out.

"There can be no traces of my blood left," he said.

The fire targeted the balled-up shirt with surgical precision, charring it down to ashes. A warm glow filled the room as Winter's magic burned away every drop of his blood on the floor, furniture and ceiling. The paper towels he had used also flamed up and vanished.

Winter turned to me, wielding the hand that held the blaze. I gulped. Blood from his wounds had sprayed all over me, but I had a serious fire phobia and human flesh that could burn.

"Don't be afraid," he said.

I was very afraid. My insides ached with an electric frenzy.

The blaze leapt from his hand and thinned into a pulsating dart of energy that attacked every molecule of his blood on my skin and clothes.

The scarlet drops vaporized one after the other. I shuddered, struggling not to freak out as his burning magic tickled me everywhere it touched.

One last hot tickle on my neck meant all his blood was gone.

God, I really hate fire magic.

Winter surveyed the place again until he was satisfied all traces of him were gone. "You have to leave this residence," he said. "Too much happened here. Destroyed spells and wards as well as supernatural essences will linger here awhile, for weeks or months maybe. It will draw others, the curious species, the dark ones."

"I'm leaving town soon," I said. "A matter of days."

His eyes told me that would be easier said than done. "Until then, you'll stay with me."

Winter strode to the door as if everything had been settled.

Faion glanced at me, concerned.

"You're coming, too," I said, grabbing my purse. "I don't want you out there alone. I'm not losing another friend this week."

I caught up with Winter at his car and pulled him aside.

"Let's be clear, this is for the safety of everyone else, not me. And I'm not taking orders from you. No chance. Nothing has changed between us."

A lazy grin formed on his lips. "That is fine."

"And Faion's staying at your place, too. Non-negotiable."

On cue, Faion walked past to check out Winter's car. "My

dude, you've been saving for thousands of years and this is the car you bought? You could have saved a table from the Age of the Renaissance and bought a damned Rolls Royce or Lambo. This some sad shit. No offense."

Faion opened the passenger door for me.

"Mr. Trice," Winter said, "this vehicle serves a purpose."

"If that purpose is humor, it does," Faion said.

I sat in the front, Faion in the back. Winter plopped down next to me in the driver's seat.

"Don't mind him," I said. "I think it's very practical."

Winter shut his door and started the car... on the second try.

"The purpose of the car is to not draw attention," Winter said. "It has a very specific, very obvious purpose."

I turned to look out the side window and fight back a grin. Almost certainly Faion was doing the same in the back seat.

Winter shifted his Civic into drive and we pulled away.

Chapter 9

We didn't know where Winter had taken us. He blindfolded us both after a while, although it was Faion's divining eyes he wanted to prevent from seeing our destination. His guarded secrets felt as loathsome to me as his many deceits.

When the blindfold came off, a sense of vague familiarity with the surroundings sparked within. I had been in that room before.

The walls were covered by dark wood panels dotted with round paintings of seascapes. A dim, orange light softened the harsh lines of a windowless room without any furniture. I shuddered, remembering the four-poster bed which I expected to pop up at any time.

This was the room in which I woke up after Winter had beaten the living daylights out of me with magic in the park. He later explained that the violent assault never happened.

Tell that to my fragile psyche. He explained it as his power of suggestion at work. I remembered it as abuse, pure and simple.

There was also this other tiny problem. I thought Winter unstable. I had seen the depths of his volcanic wrath and the extent of his duplicity. He did all this while hiding behind a veneer of solemn authority. I'd be a fool to let my guard down around him.

Winter waved his hand. The wood panels on one of the walls squeaked to the side. Metallic doors inside the wall opened in the same manner.

We stepped into the hidden room. An ultrawide monitor, a Mac notebook and stacks of papers covered the top of an enormous desk. Floor to ceiling shelves lined the side walls—some of the books on them were so old that the slightest touch might have caused them to disintegrate.

The epic journey of the written word from the paper revolution in ancient China to the digital revolution of modern-day cyberspace was starkly represented throughout the room.

"We're in your super special secret room," Faion said. "Why?"

Winter snapped his fingers and the screen came to life. "We need to plug into the Seventh Council's database."

Faion scrunched his face. "You all have a database? Do you have like Immortal IT techs and Immortal design engineers?"

"Apparently, they do," I said, sensing Winter growing tired of Faion's playful needling. "And, in fact, I'm sure he could tell us how Immortals were vital in the creation of the first motherboard."

"Indeed, I could," Winter said, "but that must wait for another day."

"Can I not be here that day?" I said.

Winter turned to Faion. "If you breathe a word of what you see to anyone, I will know, and I will come for you."

"No one will say a thing," I assured him.

"I mean, no matter what hole you hide in, young diviner," Winter continued, "you will not escape. I will husk you of your flesh and leave your skinless body for a cackle of hyenas."

"What she said," Faion said, looking faint.

"You're such a bully," I said, completely over his shit. "Have you ever heard of a toxic workplace? Because you Immortals need a few dozen HR sit-downs just to work your way up to toxic."

"Humans often speak," he said.

We waited for him to finish, then realized he already had.

Standing three feet from the desk, he held his hand flat in the air and twisted his wrist multiple times. Code sequences flowed across the blue screen, forming patterned clusters only a very skilled eye could fathom.

"This will take a while," he said. "It's searching."

Faion walked over to the bookshelves. He leaned in to read

titles that were, no doubt, in countless languages.

"Tell me," I said. "The council's plan to use technology in order to rule over the mortals, how is it progressing?"

Winter kept his focus on the screen. "Halted... temporarily."

I stepped in front of him. "Just like that?"

"It has been delayed. I know not the chain of events," he said, avoiding eye contact in order to watch rapid streams of code. "Düsternis has his reasons which he would never share with me." He motioned the screen in new ways, closing windows and clicking open icons, searching for an answer or a question or any oddity that caught his eye. "Let us focus on the fact that we have more time, for now."

Right. And I had absolutely no reason to believe that. "Can you access any information at all on Chaos in this grand database?"

"There is none."

I felt my pocket for my phone, then remembered I didn't have one.

"Then we're wasting time here," I said. "We should be out looking for Chaos."

He shook his head. "That's precisely what we should not be doing."

"Have you decided it's not Chaos, is that it? You don't know him, not the way you think you do. He's a psycho. That means you can't know him. When will you get that through your thick skull?"

"I, too, would prefer it be Chaos and not the council," Winter said with a knowing glance. "I would rather not have to go against my own faction."

I took in a sharp breath. "Are you saying I want it to be Chaos? That's the dumbest thing you've ever said and that's saying something."

"Insults are the refuge of dullards," he clapped back.

"Isn't that technically also an insult?" Faion said from a safe distance.

"This is about you, Luna," Winter continued. "You see things the way you want to see them. You always have, since you were a witchling. You ran from what you are, you ran from your boyfriends, your Oregon, and you are about to run from your country. You live in the past, in academia, in the echo chamber of your own head."

I glared at Faion who was nodding in the back of the room.

The unfeeling bastard talked on. "Yes, you want it to be Chaos, you want to project a scenario that fits a solution. This happens to beings in their first century of experience. Reality shaping, the delusion that what happens in a single feeble mind can dictate reality. You have your heart set on Chaos being the malefactor, because you think you can reason with him, that you two will talk it out like kindred souls and that he will surrender your dog-brained boyfriend back to you. It's a comedy, the Greek kind, without laughs."

I had nothing to say. I mostly wanted to punch him or at least smash him against a wall, but I also felt a little numb.

"Whatever. Just do your computer thing. I'd rather not be psychoanalyzed."

"Do me next," Faion said to chill the mood. "I'm all kinds of bent."

Winter looked away for a moment, veins throbbing in his neck. "There could be a bounty on Luna's head. They eliminate those deemed liabilities."

"Well, they must have deemed my mattress a liability. They completely gutted it. And, trust me, my mattress was completely innocent."

"She right," Faion said. "They'd have been after her guts if they wanted our girl eliminated. Not a mattress that hasn't seen a single rodeo."

Winter had learned to tune us out, which was a good thing.

His eyes darted everywhere at once as data and images flashed by on the screen with increasing speed. When recognition hit, Winter stopped his hand to freeze frame the screen. A guttural sigh escaped his lips.

"Find something?" I said.

"Not really. The grid is clean. You are not mentioned in any currently active operation."

"That's a good thing, right?" Faion said.

"Good is an imprecise word. It does not contain the clarity that you seem to think it does."

"But as far as the official Immortal network?" I asked.

"You are not a liability," Winter consented. "Everything

looks like business as usual except..."

"Except what?"

"The portal to the exile vortex has been opened."

A chill cut through my chest. "The vortex is open?"

"Not the vortex, the portal. It was briefly opened then closed again."

"Briefly?" Faion said. "How briefly? Did anything get out or... in?"

"That's it, Faion, a question of substance," Winter said.

"Can someone elaborate?" I said. "I honestly never knew if that was even a thing, a real thing, outside of supernatural studies."

Winter sat on the edge of the desk. The monitor went black. "In the time before human cities, a few Eternal Ones accumulated an abundance of raw power. The First Council of Eternal Beings beseeched them to surrender a portion of that power. Most of them complied, but for the few who resisted, a trap was set. They were captured inside enormous magnetic fields that neutralized their powers. A trial found them guilty of sedition. A parallel vortex was created and within that vortex, Eternal halls were erected to house the banished Eternals. Only the Great Eternal Magistrate and the Vortex Watch know the exact location of the vortex. The portal would never open unless to banish another Eternal, someone grown hostile to the hierarchy, whose power had burgeoned, but that is the rarest of occasions and all Immortal and Eternal Councils would have been notified."

"What do you think it means?" I said. "And how did the Seventh Council even know about it?"

"My guess is they stumbled upon it," Winter surmised. "Possibly a chain reaction causing ripples in etheric fields."

Faion crossed his arms. "Or maybe there was a whistle-blower."

None of us wanted to speak of the possible ramifications. If this was a premeditated breach opened from the inside, then for what dark purpose?

The real question was why would the Eternals sit on their hands and do nothing if this really happened? Were they so far removed from the temporal world that nothing mattered anymore? Eternals were the highest beings, and they were the keepers of all things Immortal. All councils were bound to them. They themselves had advanced up through all the stages of immortality, they were old, powerful and wise. The Great Eternal Magistrate, a.k.a. *Preceptor of Gods,* was said to be over ten thousand years old. To them, a year must feel like seconds.

"Would you put it past Chaos to be involved?" I said. "Seems like he might get a kick out of releasing deranged Eternals lusting to unleash their stifled powers upon the world. Winter, please, he's a likely suspect."

A simmering unrest stirred in his eyes. "No amount of searching will lead us to a shadow warrior who doesn't want to be found."

"That's true," Faion said, "but we diviners connect

telepathically even at great distances. Shadows are hyper sentient. Do you think you could connect with Chaos by means of telepathy?"

Winter considered the idea. "Whatever a diviner can do is surely possible for us, with proper training. Chaos would need to let his guard down, which is not likely. Even if the connection were established, we would have created a two-way street. The dark Shadow would feel me, see me, know my mind, he'd even know what I had for breakfast. He'd see you, both of you, and he'd know our mission and our plans."

Yeah, let's not do that. Hard pass.

"What about Lucia?" Faion said. "Maybe she could..."

Oh no.

Winter's deep-ocean eyes landed on mine. "Why would Faion think I know this person, Luna?"

I shrugged. "He's obviously just babbling."

"No, that was no random babble. He mentioned a name. *Lucia.* She clearly possesses abilities. I want to hear of this woman."

No way out. Faion looked sheepish, like he'd swallowed a bug.

"Lucia is Lily's mother. She is a human and an unwitting player in all these sordid affairs. Chaos created an open channel through her where he could create energy. Under his control, she was the one who attacked me in the parking garage. When Chaos came looking for me, I insisted he release her, which he did. She doesn't remember a thing."

Winter went stone cold, obviously pissed at not being told sooner. Screw him, he was hardly the poster boy for vital information sharing.

He scowled and clenched his fists. "What else have you kept from me?"

"Nothing. I needed to keep Lucia away from all this. She deserved that much. It was my business. Not yours, not the Council's."

"And you've played into Chaos's hands no doubt," he said with a huff.

"Ah, so we have that in common now," I quickly said.

He shook his head. "What a daft little witch you can be... did you really think he no longer has full access to her?"

Not specifically, but any basic could be accessed by Chaos. Duh.

Winter rose to his feet. "I lose patience with neophyte beings. It is to be expected." He sighed. "I'll let the program comb through all databases on the Immortal network. Maybe there will be an irregularity. In the meantime, notify your friend. We'll be paying her mom a visit."

I counted on my fingers. "One, I don't have a phone. Two, Lucia is out of town today. Three, if this really needs to happen, there's a New Year's Eve party at her house tomorrow. We plan to attend."

"I'm her date," Faion interjected. "I got this wine-colored velvet blazer. We going to make an entrance, you feel me?"

"You're going with her out of sympathy, I suspect," Winter said. "We all know you would have more fun at a livelier gala, Mr. Trice."

"That's kind of true," Faion said out of the side of his mouth.

"Oh my god, dude," I said. "I'm right here."

"Sorry, Sophie," my so-called-friend said. "I can't lie. I am a man with options. And there's a literal gala. Scary dude on point with that."

"I am to be your plus one," Winter stated. He opened a drawer and handed me an old flip cell phone with an antenna.

"Did you rob a museum?" I said, flipping open the phone.

"It's a burner phone," Winter said. "It can't be traced or compromised. You and Faion can stay at my place tonight. I've a previous engagement."

"Booty call," Faion said, coughing the words into his shoulder.

"It's a private matter," Winter said.

A private matter? Apparently, those were for everyone but me.

Chapter 10

WINTER HANDED LUCIA A bottle of Dom Perignon champagne with a dry smile and marched straight into the living room in his navy-blue cashmere turtleneck and gray slacks. There were seemingly no clothes that could diminish his fierce masculinity.

I didn't expect my date on New Year's Eve to be so old. Ancient, even. My Immortal companion had agreed he would only observe and not use any interrogation methods, but his promises were interpretive at best.

Lily, Lucia and I stood in the hallway, staring at him walk away.

"Another one, Sophie? You've certainly been busy," Lucia said. She looked at the Dom Perignon bottle. "Expensive taste too."

"Mamá, that's not her boyfriend, it's her uncle."

Lily was enjoying this.

Lucia raised her eyebrows. "Uncle? Isn't he a bit young?"

Young? It was hard not to laugh. "He's not my uncle."

"That's right," Lil said. "He's her uncle's friend. Señor Sugar Daddy."

Cute, Lily. Any cuter and I'll dump the fish tank on your head.

Lucia tilted her head. "Well, he seems like a nice man and a very curious choice for a date on New Year's Eve, Sophie."

"What's curious?" Lily said. "Little Miss Perfect wants to jump his bones."

Winter lingered near the living room's entrance and leaned back to glance at me. Had he heard us? Probably, his senses were animal like.

"Lily, your manners," Lucia instructed her daughter, then grabbed me gently by the shoulders. "I hope you understand the value of safe sex, Sophie. With multiple sexual partners, condoms are a must."

Oh-my-gawd. When I kill Lily, it will be slow and painful.

"You girls have fun," Lucia said. "Everyone's here. I better go be a good little hostess."

I took Lily's hand as Lucia sauntered off. "Who's everyone?"

"Two of Lucia's colleagues from college with their spouses, a couple neighborhood families and an eccentric lady from Costa Rica. I'm not sure how they met, but Lucia has taken her under her wing, so to speak."

"When you say *eccentric*?"

"Whisper into her ear and you'll hear echo. Spews utter nonsense."

Okay then.

Lily pouted. "Did you really have to bring the turtleneck Viking along? I thought the idea was to go out after midnight."

"We are," I assured her.

"I mean, I might want to hook up. No guy in their right mind will approach us with Uncle Beefcake at our table. He looks like a preppy pimp."

Okay, that was funny. "He's obviously not invited, Lil. You spaz."

"Maybe he'll make a pass at Lucia. He could be my new stepdad."

It wouldn't be her first Shadow Warrior.

"Gross," I said. "I don't want to think of that."

"I know," she said, "because you want him."

I punched her shoulder. "Are you done?"

"Hey," she said, a little shocked.

"Can we please mingle?" I said.

"Yeah, fine. You don't need to get violent."

"It was a love tap."

Lily shook her head. "You're a total freak, Collinsworth. So, why did you bring him?"

"Jonas asked me out."

This stunned her. "He did not."

"He totally did, but in a respectful manner," I said, enjoying the various shades of bewilderment on Lily's face.

"He's all kinds of hot, but Sophie," Lily said, then dragged me to the living room doorway, "that posture is too much, like a PE teacher, an elementary school PE teacher. Uptight and a little predatorial."

Winter wasn't there, but I could not deny her take. Instead, my eyes fell on the person that had to be the eccentric lady. She wore a worn-out tuxedo, galoshes, 3D glasses and held a pink umbrella.

I mean... I'm not even mad. Wow.

Lucia walked to the kitchen with an empty tray. I could hear her talking to someone and my gut told me the rest. Entering the bright kitchen, I saw Lucia handing Winter a tray full of mouth-drooling, savory canapés.

"Jonas offered to help," Lucia said joyfully.

I forced a smile. "He does like to get involved."

"Lucia has been regaling me with stories of Latin American legends," Winter said. "Grand stories of beautiful wild women with magical powers who roam the forest, sucking the life out of men foolish enough to follow them."

An obvious false equivalency that he thought was clever.

"Las Ciguapas," I said. "I've read about them."

He narrowed his eyes to show disbelief. "You have?"

"Yeah, Caribbean folklore was a pod within the Latin American folklore course at school. Wasn't that a Dominican myth?"

"It was," Lucia said, "but it is not a myth. There are still sightings."

This amused us all for different reasons.

"I want all myths to be true," I said. "I loved how those women had backward feet so if men tried to follow, they would never know which way the Ciguapas were going. The men were clueless even then."

"The world of the past," Winter went on, licking his lips. "These stories fascinate me, telling us details about people living a thousand years ago. Each of us can taste just a little bit of history, almost as if we were there."

Intolerable. His self-love was nauseating. The fact that Lucia was charmed almost made me sick.

"Folktales do not report history, rather the creative subconscious," I said, trying to kick him off his double meaning express train.

He grinned in agreement. "So true, Sophie, themes and details recur all over the world through all times. If we didn't know better, it would seem there was someone there all along connecting the stories."

"God," Lucia said.

Oh, brother. This man.

"Exactly," Winter said. "Some kind of god, a charming one no doubt."

God, if you're out there, please strike me down.

I turned to Lucia. "Let me help, too. Which tray should I grab?"

"We have it under control," she said, then turned to Winter. "Jonas, could you be a dear and take those canapés out for the guests?"

Winter bowed with old world gallantry, then left with the tray.

"All your boyfriends are polite and intelligent," Lucia said, "but I think Jonas might not be a good fit for you."

Please, no. Don't tell me she thought he was a good fit for her. What was it with Lucia and deranged Immortals?

"Not a boyfriend," I assured her. "Lily likes to push my buttons."

"She does that to both of us," Lucia said with a wink, "but I see things that you girls cannot. It comes with experience, with years. That man looks at you in a certain kind of way. I've seen it before. It's possessive, territorial."

"He's harmless," I said even though he was anything but.

"Okay, if you say so, but please, my dove, be careful."

I needed a warning about Winter's possessiveness about as much as I needed e-coli in my lettuce. "And what about you, Lucia?" I said. "When was the last time you dated anyone?"

She smiled. "Touché. I guess I earned that. There is such a thing as being too careful. The truth is, since my divorce, I have devoted myself to Lily and my work. Don't get me wrong, there were a few forgettable guys, but no one who grabbed my imagination." She stopped to ponder.

Are you sure about that, Lucia?

She handed me a jug of lemonade.

"Here you are, now you can help," she said.

The partygoers had all settled into engaged conversations. As soon as I set the jug of lemonade down on the serving table, Winter placed his hand on the small of my back and led me down the hallway to the sunroom.

Moonlight poured through the all-glass walls. Counters everywhere were overfull with empty pots, jars, glass tubes, and gardening tools. A sofa bed with amethyst purple cushions, a stack of unused flowerpots, and green metal shelves packed with gardening books sat against the one brick wall.

"There's a definite hold on Lucia's aura," Winter said, pacing the room, "but it seems dormant."

My head spun at his assertion. "Chaos still has access to Lucia?"

"He's not accessing her. Not now, but he made it so he could reopen that pathway with a snap of his fingers."

Immortals are total shit. He left it there for insurance.

"Of course, he did," I said, defeated.

I stepped over a trowel and padded to the glass door. Lucia's garden breathed heavily under the moonlight. Fruit trees surrounded the manicured lawn. Clumps of carnations, dahlias and begonias bloomed in flower beds. Rose bushes budded in the back. Green vines climbed up pickets.

The moonshine entered my pores through the glass. I breathed in the green elemental energy. My powers ebbed and flowed in my every cell, invigorating me.

"Can you open Lucia's connective path?" I asked him.

"If I wanted," he confirmed. "That channel would lead me to Chaos. He would not know it was me, but it would come at a cost to the woman."

I figured as much. "Be more specific and her name is Lucia."

He picked up a poorly made ceramic pot. Cartoonish flowers and Lily's name were painted on the pot. She must have made it for her mother as a child.

"Using Lucia's connective channel to connect with Chaos could be devastating. She will remember everything, all at once. It could rupture her conscience. She could be left schizophrenic or worse."

"Oh," I said, "then we're not doing that."

In his eyes, I saw spreading darkness. "Even if that was avoided, the telepathic command Chaos had over Lucia would be renewed and it could never be reversed. Only the master of the spell could shut it down."

"Lucia would become a pawn in his sadistic games again."

Winter nodded. "That's the best-case scenario."

I shivered. "And the worst?"

"Her mind becomes non-responsive, completely."

"Like my mother, locked in a vegetative state. We'll find another way."

"Are you sure?"

"Winter? Yeah, I'm sure," I said. "Was that even a question?"

"So be it," he said, then turned and walked away.

I dashed after him, grabbing his arm before he went out the front door.

"What are you doing?" I said.

"Please, make my excuses to the lovely hostesses. I'm afraid I've exhausted every reserve I had stored for small talk the last few centuries."

"You're joking?"

"I wish I was," he said. "When basics chitter chatter it's so grating, like stone scraping across hide."

"It's New Year's Eve," I said and immediately regretted it.

Winter furrowed his brow. "You want me to stay?"

With dread, I realized that part of me did want him to stay. I wanted him to be next to me when the year changed, because left to my own devices, I'd probably get drunk on wine which always led to wishy washy confessions with Lily, who would then pepper me with a million questions.

"I'll stay if you want me to."

His voice was breathy and soft. The space between us felt too small and a little asphyxiating. I stared into his eyes. They were hungry, savage eyes—you couldn't hide from them no matter how you tried. Could there possibly be a well of loneliness deep inside him? Inside all Immortals?

Lucia's words rang inside my skull. *Possessive, territorial...* add lethal and manipulative to the mix and we'd be all set, Lucia.

I reconsidered. "No, a new year, even calendars themselves, must be meaningless to your kind. I won't keep you.

I'd rather you apply your time to finding Emmet."

He put his hands in his pockets and nodded. "We'll celebrate the turn of the century then, when all these people have moved on."

As he turned to go, I felt an odd pang in my stomach.

"Jonas, wait," I said. "I appreciate your help. I know you don't have to."

He leaned in, his lips inches from mine. "As always. I will be with you in the shadows until you've come into your own."

Winter was gone before my heart could take its next beat. A massive sigh escaped my lungs. Had I been holding my breath?

When I turned to go back to the party, I found the eccentric woman standing rigidly in the living room doorway. She was staring at me.

The 3D glasses were gone, the pink umbrella was closed and serving as a peculiar walking stick. She looked older now. Her small eyes swam inside puffy dark circles. Her gray tangled hair and thin lifeless lips coupled with her sharp wrinkles made her face appear chiseled in stone.

She started speaking Spanish, or something like it—both her strange accent and the frantic speed at which she spoke made it hard to understand.

"Lo siento!" I said. "I don't speak Spanish. No hablo español."

She didn't seem to care. What she was saying meant far

more to her than anything I had to say. She kept at it, talking wildly, gesticulating.

Then she slowed down and articulated two words carefully. The look in her eyes sent chills right through me. Then she spoke again, slower.

"Este es el *apocalipsis* del *infierno*," she said.

This is the apocalypse from hell.

Huh. I think I'll have that drink now.

Chapter 11

"Yugoslavia is about to capitulate!" The gaming laptop bounced in Faion's lap as he clapped excitedly.

I stepped closer to get a better look at the strange map on the screen. There were names of countries no longer existing, like the Soviet Union, and some that I never knew existed, like Manchukuo and the Guangxi Clique, whatever that meant.

"What game is that?" I said.

"You never heard of this game? Sad. It's only the best strategy game ever made. It's called Hearts of Iron IV. You control a country in World War II. Dude, you manage military, politics, supply lines, everything. It's dope."

"How can you just switch gears like that?" I said, wishing I could forget all the real world doom my monkey brain kept obsessing over.

"Less talking," he said as he went back to his game.

This was not how I wanted to spend New Year's Day, being shushed.

Lily convinced me to go to the Altitude Sky Lounge last night. Even after ringing in the new year, the bar remained packed. It was almost worth the cramped quarters to catch its breathtaking rooftop view.

We emptied our tequila shots into Corona beer bottles. I remembered having at least three. I should have had a hellish hangover this morning and, honestly, I'd prefer that to constantly mulling over every detail about Emmet's disappearance, but no. I didn't even get tipsy, nothing, zero, zilch.

I'd have to ask Winter about that. Alcohol used to hit me hard. Was immortality something I had grown into? Did it mean I'd never have the luxury of drowning my sorrows in a few nice shots of Tequila?

Lily, however, got so wrecked she sent away every cute guy who asked to sit with us. She sang the national anthem and *God Save the Queen*, both out of tune, all the way home. At some point, she belched so loud, the Uber driver pulled over fearing she would throw up in his car. She asked me to take her to her apartment instead of Lucia's house where her roommates were having their own "after bar" party. I did, but I now realized it was a horrendous idea.

I rested my arm on the back of the velvety cream couch. It was hard to believe I had bled out on this couch not long ago when Winter slashed into me with a dagger to prove

I couldn't be killed. *Good times.* But now, if not for Faion crouched over his laptop, you'd think the couch had just come out of its plastic wrap.

In fact, the whole apartment was showroom quality. Nothing betrayed that a human had ever lived in the pristine condo. Then again, Winter was far from human.

He had keyed his elaborate wards to Faion and me so they would tolerate our presence. That meant we could come and go as we pleased without disturbing them. They still guarded Winter's office for him only. If we so much as dared to walk within five feet of the office door, the wards shadowed our every move, unsure of our intentions, white and red lines glowing around the doorframe like laser beams, ready to strike.

I had grown weary of this cat and mouse game. I had provoked the kidnappers by shuttering their blood spell and blowing up their wards, yet they hadn't shown their faces.

There had not been a word from Winter since he left Lucia's party. I felt like a caged wild cat in a zoo. It drove me batty that I had spent two days locked away in a warded Immortal enclave while Emmet's fate hung in the balance. We should be out there looking for him, turning over every last stone until we unearthed these soul swallowers and their dark lord.

If I didn't do something soon, I'd lose my mind.

I waited until Faion was wholly absorbed by an invasion in his World War II game before I grabbed my purse and jacket.

I could have walked right out the front door and he would have never raised his head.

Dudes and their video games.

"Hey, Imperial conqueror," I said, waving a hand under his eyes. "I'm going to bounce."

"Hold on," he said, pausing the game. "Where you going? The old dude said to wait."

"Yeah, I don't care. Sorry not sorry. I'm done sitting on my hands."

"Luna, you'll just piss him off. I mean, we have no leads. Nada. What could we possibly accomplish on our own?"

I opened my mouth and then clamped it shut again.

The wards hummed and hissed. My body tingled from head to toe as if the air had been suddenly electrified.

"You feel that?" I asked Faion.

He set his laptop on the coffee table and nodded.

Tendrils of smoke oozed inside from the edges of the doorframe. The wards had been compromised. The door shuddered. The handle swayed. Whoever was outside was not Winter. His wards would have no visible reaction to him. He'd just walk through like a normal tenant.

"Faion, get down," I shouted.

I readied an energy bolt in my right hand, raw power swelling in my core, and shot it at the door as soon as it opened.

Kirsi raised her sword, driving it straight into the bolt of energy and deflecting it with a mighty jolt. The bolt zoomed straight back at me. Out of pure instinct, I blocked it with another energy wave.

I never even had a chance to think.

The bolt collided with the energy wave, sparking combustible magic in the air which burst and then swirled its way to the floor like glittering confetti.

All three of us watched the confetti vanish.

"That could have been us," Kirsi said. "Way too close for comfort."

Once upon a time, Kirsi had been a Valkyrie—a warrior goddess of the Nordic pantheon who shepherded souls through battle or into the afterlife. Now she was a very old Immortal who had helped me recover after the battle of the metamorphic night when I threw myself between Chaos and Winter.

"I see why swords can come in handy," I quipped, although still rattled that if not for my instinct, we would have been scorched and skewered. I'd survive, but Faion would not.

Kirsi laughed. Beauty wasn't what she was about, but few would ever turn away from her if she walked past. She had big, almond-shaped brown eyes and luscious, auburn curls that were now pulled back into a ponytail. Her face radiated a laid-back ease but, at the same time, a *takes-no-shit-from-nobody* attitude. Her toned legs were wrapped tightly in black leather pants and her arms in a fashion fitted biker jacket. The word for her was *striking*.

Faion gulped as if he'd forgotten what team he played on.

Kirsi raised an eyebrow. "That's something I would pay to see. A lunar witch wielding a sword."

Faion snorted. I ignored them both. They wouldn't be laughing if I found that magic mist horse, would they?

"And this must be the diviner." Kirsi shared a smile with Faion. "Tell me, insightful one, can you see into my future?"

"No, but with my own eyes I can see the present and in the here and now we done pissed off a witch and she throws fireballs when she ornery."

Kirsi chuckled. "Magistrate Winter warned me of her temper." She extended a hand to Faion. "They call me Kirsi, Immortal warrior and guard of the Seventh Council Seal."

"I'm Faion," he said, taking her hand. "Love the Bougie title. Don't know what it means but it's got swag."

"Why, thank you," Kirsi said. "It's a cool gig."

Is it me or was that BFFs at first sight?

"Winter's not here," I told Kirsi. "Been gone since last night. We have no clue when he's expected to return."

"It was Winter who sent me," she said. "He wanted me to deliver this."

She handed me a manila envelope. There was no writing on the outside and inside I found a printed google map and two notes. The first note was just an address. The second was a short message.

"The database search spat out a clue. Meet me at 9:00 am local time at the marked location on the map. On foot once you

reach La Mejilla Street. Leave the diviner at home. Approach the building from the east."

The map was of Tijuana, Mexico. Winter wanted to meet in an eastside neighborhood, outside of a shop called *Palacio de Taxidermia*.

A taxidermist? He didn't think someone had embalmed Emmet, did he? Sure, he often turned into a gigantic wolf, but c'mon!

"He wants to meet in Mexico," I said. "Me only. It doesn't say why."

"He's there already, keeping..." Kirsi stopped in mid-sentence. "Look, you should trust him. If he says you have to meet him, you should go."

"Everyone has to jump when he snaps his fingers. I know the drill."

Alone again in Mexico with Winter? The last time we poked around down there, I got poked, literally, by a morph dagger in the heart. And that was only the second biggest shock to my system that night. The other shock cut much deeper and was not something from which I could ever recover, the soul crushing discovery of what I actually was.

I eyed the second note. It was a local San Diego address. I knew the street, an upper-class neighborhood near the east end of campus.

"What's this?" I said.

Kirsi eyed the note in my hand. "Ken Groshek is staying there."

"So, Winter just spilled all my secrets to you, didn't he?"

Those were my secrets. They weren't his to share.

Kirsi weighed the proper response. "I owe Winter a great deal. He knows I would never betray him. And I would never betray you, Luna."

Apparently, everybody owed Winter something. Did he help people? *Yes.* Would he call in those favors? *Hell yes.* Typical egomaniacal brilliance.

Kirsi smiled tenderly. It was hard to believe she was an Immortal. "Luna, I consider you a friend. I nursed you after the metamorphic battle because I wanted that job, not because I was asked. I love strong women. You stand your ground. You don't back down and you are driven by your heart."

"Couldn't he send an email and a few attachments?" I insisted. "Perhaps a quick phone call?"

I saw a flickering hesitation in her eyes. "Düsternis has imposed a moratorium on digital communications effective today. Winter abides by that edict and wishes to remain inconspicuous."

"Even Immortals get hacked," Faion said. "It's them *Somali* pirates, they off the boats now and at the keyboard. *I'm the coder now.*"

We both just stared at Faion. Without a word we turned from him, and I walked Kirsi to the door. The wards hummed, then turned red before darting away to let Kirsi out. Apparently, they were not completely sure about her.

Once outside, Kirsi turned back. "He has your back, Luna. Count on that."

I counted on myself. I learned that the hard way. Instead, I would concentrate on the fact that Winter had uncovered a clue. I'd put my energies there.

Back inside, I found Faion standing with crossed arms. "I know what you're thinking," he said, "because I'm thinking the same thing."

"What am I thinking?"

"That something is off. It's all too convenient."

I agreed so far. "And?"

Faion nodded. "You know, my little moon baby. You're thinking Mr. Winter Wonderland might have orchestrated the whole damn thing."

"No, I'm not thinking that," I said. "For what possible purpose?"

"Oh, shit," Faion said, suddenly concerned. "That means you blind and if you blind to all this maybe you want all this. He's all about you and maybe you about him. May the world survive because you two some strange bedfellows."

Suddenly I felt tired. I closed my eyes and took a few deep breaths. "Your blathering nonsense is exhausting me."

"Okay, but don't nobody say Faion Trice didn't warn you."

Chapter 12

THE TERRAIN WAS ROUGH and dry. Huge piles of dirt ran along the sides of the gravel road. Abandoned tenements loomed above my head like skeletal remains of giant prehistoric animals.

The taxi driver dropped me at the end of La Calle Mejilla and I walked the rest of the way. The *Palacio de Taxidermia* should show up at any moment, assuming I wasn't completely lost.

Orientation skills were never my strongest suit. I took the map out of my backpack to study it one more time. At night, I had the benefit of the moon's guidance, but during daytime, I had to think twice to tell east from west.

I wished Winter's message had included more details. As it was, I didn't even know how long I was supposed to stay in Tijuana or what I should have packed. The only things

I brought along were dry snacks, a book, a sweater and the note I managed to obtain from Ken Groshek.

Early in the morning, I took a detour heading to the Mexican border. The address Winter had provided for Emmet's father led me to a carriage style home fronted by a small yard, white rose bushes and a large stone fountain.

The careful hope that I saw on his face when he opened the door made my stomach plunge. I didn't want to play with his emotions, so I excluded mention of any possible clues in Mexico.

He was more than willing to relinquish the note that had been nailed to Emmet's door. I promised to contact him as soon as I had any news at all.

Barely more than two hours later, I was walking the deserted streets at the east edge of Tijuana. I turned onto a narrow dirt path lined with dense foliage that eventually opened onto a natural cul-de-sac.

The Palacio stood amidst discarded debris and haggard trees topped by ominous, decaying branches.

I assessed the area for signs of Winter. A gray rat the size of a rabbit shot out from behind a tree and dashed across the path. Somewhere to the right, two ravens fluttered away croaking.

Picking my way down the path to the *Palacio de Taxidermia*, I kept my gait measured and quiet. The Palacio was a two-story, white stucco building fronted by three arches that framed a narrow patio and supported a balcony. Chunks of stucco had peeled off, revealing old, wood-brown bricks. A corner of the roof had been torn and blown away in some windstorm of the past.

A metallic, clicking sound snapped behind me. I heaved forward when the shot rang out and landed hard on all fours. Excruciating pain erupted in my left knee which bore the brunt of the fall.

I crawled the few feet to the Palacio and dove inside the middle arch, throwing a sizzling energy shield around me. A second shot fired, hitting the back of my leg. Searing pain ripped through my calf. I screamed.

My head reeled with confusion. Bullets shouldn't be able to penetrate my energy shield. Not that I had tested the theory before, but shields were supposed to withstand any attacks by handheld basic weapons, at least for a while.

I caught a glimpse of a hooded figure perched in an old tree. I slithered my way behind the arch column. A third shot sliced the air and hit my other calf, this one coming from a different direction.

Clenching my teeth, I drew in more elemental power to bolster my shield.

An onslaught of bullets exploded in a flash of flickering sparks, thudding into the walls behind me, shredding the arch pillars.

I ducked, covering my head with my arms, not trusting my shield. My legs had begun to heal but I was in no hurry to feel more burning pain.

The double doors of the Palacio swung open. Winter rushed out taking fire from every direction. Bullets cut through him, blasting him back against the door.

I scurried to him, staying low. The assault rifles opened fire again. My ears rang. Breaking glass and splintering wood stabbed into my flesh like hot pins, then a bullet exploded into the center of my back. Any resistance shield would have been useless against such an assault.

I went down. My spine crumbled, my insides burned and I gasped for air, but instead of air my lungs drowned in blood.

Winter stumbled to his feet and raised his hands defiantly. A new round of thunderous shots tracked Winter when the bullets froze in midair, inches from Winter's extended palms, as if stopped by an invisible barrier. The bullets dropped harmlessly to the ground.

I struggled to draw air into my lungs. Everything hurt at once. I reached out and grabbed onto Winter's blood-stained pants.

He removed my hand with a firm grip and sprinted down the gravel road after the shooters. Within seconds, he vanished from view.

I tried to get onto my feet but found it impossible to move. I was losing blood too fast. My healing process was compromised. I stayed still, bringing every spark of energy to the bullet holes.

From a distance came the blood-curdling sound of brutal impact, then silence.

Total silence. Not even the birds chirped.

I was fading away when I saw Winter's legs marching back toward me. He had healed completely whereas I moaned through thin breaths, trying to expel bullets from my wounds.

He was far ahead of me in the immortality game. How many centuries would it take me to get there?

"You are stronger than you know," he said softly, almost lovingly.

"It hurts," I said between sobs.

"I know. We all feel that pain. Learn to accept it."

A few bullets fell out and my body started to swell in healing power.

"What the fuck was that?" I asked, wiping tears from my eyes.

"A welcoming party," he said. "They clearly don't want us to see inside."

"Are they the freaks who took Emmet?"

"Don't think so." He used a handkerchief to wipe blood from my face.

"Why don't you think so? What don't I know?"

"We know there's at least one Immortal involved. They wouldn't have sent men with guns to try to stop a shadow warrior."

"Unless the Immortal has a chaotic sense of humor," I said. "Get it? *Chaotic*... see what I did there?"

He nodded, almost sympathetically, at my wordplay.

"I'm even funnier when I have more blood," I said, still delirious from blood loss and his gentle pampering.

"Even funnier?"

"Stop being a mean man," I said. "You have to admit, our boy Chaos is kind of a fan of the *failed mission for sake of annoyance* concept."

He considered my eyes for a long while. "Those were ghost guards. They are neither human nor supernatural. They were created specifically to guard Eternal archives and vaults. Normal magic is useless against them because they didn't derive from the magic world. They weren't here for us, Luna. They protect what's inside and I have yet to discover what that might be."

"Perhaps a pot of gold?" I said. "Or, maybe, some lucky charms."

"Good," he said. "You're replacing blood. That was a bit funnier."

"You don't know funny," I said. "But why this place? It's no one's first choice for anything. It's an eternal dump at best."

"It did come as a surprise to find them guarding an abandoned taxidermy museum of all places," he said. "I guess being the last place was the point."

"So, we're screwed," I said. "Our presence here will soon reach the ears of the Immortal Magistrate Courts and beyond."

He looked away into the distance. "It only reached about

fifty feet in that direction. They have been rendered silent."

"Oh," I said. What else could I say?

He rose and walked to the door. He glanced back. "It's now or never."

I forced myself up. I inhaled the putrid air. I took my sweater out of my backpack. It had somehow made it through with only one bullet hole in it.

"How about *never*? I mean, that's the Eternals' turf?" I said, pulling the sweater on over my head.

"The whole world's their turf," he said, fastening his gaze on me. "But, hey, if you want to forget about saving the smug wolf, we can stop now."

I was just saying. Sheesh. I knew we were going in.

With a grunt I followed him into the Palacio. Two standing Egyptian mummies and four human skulls on spikes decorated the anteroom which opened onto a large hall. We were greeted by grim-looking sculpted busts on pedestals, most likely representations of Eternals and Magistrates. To the left, a row of glass cases sported various small creatures of the Deep Down in odd poses, several of them extinct.

Off to the right, embalmed animals of unnatural size stared menacingly at the void—grizzly bears, lions, wolves, tigers, hyenas...

I swallowed hard. These weren't animals per se, they were shapeshifters captured in their beastly forms while trying to escape.

We walked through a low doorway and came into a dark

room. Winter snapped his fingers. Supple light filled the space, framing objects in the room with sharp contours.

The collection of medical equipment and devices, including imaging machines, surgical instruments, infusion pumps, monitors and an operating table with a real body lying on it, shook me.

The body was pale and dry as if drained of all its blood. A surgical incision cut across the front from the throat down to the navel. The skin had been peeled to the side, revealing bones and a deep cavity where the gut should have been. In fact, the entire torso was empty of organs.

Winter opened a freezer door in the back of the room. Bodies in various stages of decomposition rolled out. There were monsters with two heads, others with tentacles on their backs, and still more with long sharp claws.

There was a troglodyte and more humanoid variants, and there was a woman that looked, well, human. A gray dress covered her emaciated body and her eyes were left wide open. I placed my palm on her face to close her eyes when I sensed raw, elemental energy twist my insides.

The dead woman had been a lunar witch.

"It's appalling," Winter said. "They've been conducting experiments."

Rage fueled my magic, forcing it to rise. My aura quaked about me. Glass tubes cracked. The floor trembled. I clenched my fists to prevent a dangerous escalation that would burst out and take down the building.

"Relax," Winter said. "We don't know what lurks inside these walls."

I could still hear energy roaring in my head. "Is this why they want Emmet? And me? For their sick experiments?"

He ignored me and motioned to a door in the back.

It was a basic office. A moldy odor hit our nostrils. Winter opened a window, disturbing the dust particles on the desk and file cabinets.

"What is the actual reason we're here?" I asked. "You never said."

"A notation in the database. There were to be a number of shapeshifters transported to the Palacio before being transferred to an unknown jurisdiction." He dusted the desk with his right hand.

"Transferred by whom?"

"That's also unknown."

I rolled my eyes. "Unknown seems to be our only lead."

"Stop whining and look for clues."

"Is mold a clue?"

"Look for anything that connects in any way to the wolf boy."

I glanced about the room. There were filing cabinets on two walls. We split up the cabinets to search. I opened a top drawer. I stroked the backs of the tan folders inside and pulled one out. I leafed through pages of sketches and diagrams that meant nothing to me.

Looking for something when you didn't have even the

foggiest idea of what you're looking for was difficult.

Winter started on the other side, opening drawers in rapid succession, dumping their contents on the floor.

I heaved a sigh. "Our fingerprints will be all over this shit."

"Your fingerprints are the last thing you should be worried about."

He had a point. My etheric field was the real beacon for our enemies.

I copied him, yanking drawers open and rushing through the contents until I came upon a file with *E.G.* printed on its tab.

Sweat glistened on my fingers as I opened the file. Emmet's passport photo was clipped onto a page with text written underneath in what I assumed were letters of the Greek alphabet.

"Winter," I said, handing him the text. "I have no idea what it says."

He fixed me with a knowing stare. "That's because it's ancient Greek."

"Please, tell me you can read ancient Greek."

His eyes sparked. "Let's just say that Aristotle and I enjoyed more than a few drunken symposiums."

"Aristotle was your drinking buddy?"

He grinned, then turned serious.

"What is it?"

"According to this, a group of shifters were moved to a holding facility outside Whitehorse, Yukon."

"In Canada?" I said. "Why do I sense there's more to that?"

Winter hesitated. "The Fifth Council meets in Whitehorse next week. It's our only Canadian Magistrate Court."

"The Fifth Council?"

"The council that monitors human activity and online trends to ensure that basics never even begin to form the idea that we exist."

"It looks like they've graduated to kidnapping," I suggested.

"Or that's what someone wants us to think," he said. "Either way, there's only one way to find out."

"We go to northern Canada."

"I will fly to Whitehorse. Alone," he said.

"That's probably exactly what they want."

He considered my words. "I'll bring Kirsi as backup."

"Why is it always Kirsi?"

My question revealed something to him. "Luna, do you really think she was chosen randomly as your guard against the morphs?" He spoke slowly as if to a child. "I chose her because she is one of the few I can trust. She's also a friend."

"A friend? Is that Winter speak for yet another conquest?"

"Must you revert to jealousy every time like a schoolgirl? Although it may be flattering, it is not dignified."

"Jealous of you?" I said. "Dream on, dude. I'm worried about possible complications if you two have a moment and then have a fall out. I wouldn't want a lover's quarrel to ruin our mission. Emmet's life is at stake."

Bringing Emmet up might have been a mistake. The only reason Winter was willing to help at all was because he wanted me to owe him, or because he maybe thought he owed me, or because of some grand manipulation he was planning. His motivation didn't matter. What mattered was that we save Emmet and derail the diabolical Immortal conspiracy.

"No need to worry. We're both adults."

Did he mean unlike me? "Kirsi needs a vacation. I'm going."

He grinned. "As you wish."

Now it all made sense. He knew I would offer. Of course, he did. That was the entire reason why Kirsi was involved at all and I had walked straight into it yet again. Winter had maneuvered me like a chess piece, so I'd volunteer to be his sidekick, the very thing I had vowed never to do.

Chapter 13

Heavy clouds obscured the night sky, cloaking the half moon. Strong gusts bent tree branches as falling leaves whizzed by in a frenzy. I pushed the apartment door open with my boot and flipped the light switch. I'd been so restless since I got back to San Diego I needed to apply my nervous energy to some manual task, or I'd lose my mind.

If it were up to me, I'd have flown straight to Whitehorse after Tijuana, but Winter had to use some nuance with the Seventh Council to cover for his absence before taking off again. Apparently, it was a time for the Immortal councils to be in session and his absence was conspicuous.

I slid out of my jacket and carefully sat on my ruined sofa. It'd take inhuman effort to order my place, but it was better than being trapped at Winter's condo, sulking. Faion had decided to return to his dorm room. I made him promise to call right away if he noticed a single unusual thing.

I decided to start with my most cherished possession—my books. I got down on my knees and collected the least damaged hardcovers first, stacking them in even piles.

Someone whistled outside my window. I stopped working to listen, then returned to my task. Another, louder whistle stopped me cold.

I slid open the window to look outside. I was on the second floor. The ground below was clear, a row of green shrubs swaying in the wind.

In the apartment windows across the street, dim lights glowed.

Chaos swung forth right in front of my face like a nightmarish shadow. His fingers somehow clawed onto the window frame. He grinned.

I shrieked and backed away, shocked to my core.

Chaos leapt through the window and landed on the gutted sofa.

My throat went dry. It was the first time I saw him indoors. He looked huge in my cramped lodging—not only tall, but powerful. His hulking arms and thick neck felt primitive and virile. His eyelashes were long and his gaze piercing. His hair was darker than I remembered, and his black jeans and black trench coat created a slick impression like he was a movie hitman.

"I love what you've done with the place," he said, running his fingers back through his long hair. "Edgy décor...

has a Bohemian dope fiend vibe."

My heartbeat jackhammered, but I did not run. "Yeah, well, my interior decorator was a real douchebag."

Chaos laughed in approval. He had a giddy, barely masculine laugh.

"There was a more elegant time when college girls dared not use such vulgar dictums," he said.

"Only a man would view such patriarchal times as elegant," I said, ready to drop some truth on this brutish relic of a man.

He stopped laughing and studied me. "There is an unusual aura that rises from you when your temper rises. Curious."

"I am a woman, not an object of curiosity."

"You are a woman," he said. "Indeed, as well as many other things."

"So, did you bring the proof we talked about? Or were you too busy with the usual tasks of hijacking women's minds, kidnapping supernatural creatures and cutting up their bodies for pointless experiments?"

He moved closer. "What sickly fascinations have rooted in your mind?"

I backed away, giving myself room to maneuver if I had to fight.

"Isn't that your thing? Messing with lives out of deranged boredom?"

Keeping my cool was excruciatingly difficult. His eyes bored holes in my brain, short-circuiting my thought process. If I brought up Emmet, he'd for sure deny the whole thing and I'd be out of moves. The best strategy was to let things play out.

He circled me. I shuffled to the right to stand near the kitchen, so I would not find myself cornered or pressed up against a wall with no escape.

Chaos glanced about the place, intrigued. "What happened here?"

So, we're playing a game of pretend. Great.

"A failed tryst of some sort?" he probed. "Jealousy broke out during a ménage à trois?"

"Madman," I said.

Wicked glee shaped his grin. "What are you hiding, pumpkin?"

I raised my right fist to his chin. Energy sizzled between my knuckles.

"A nice high-voltage treat. Want to try a little zap?"

Amused, he flashed perfect white teeth. "No foreplay, Luna. I am here to solve a riddle, the one you won't share."

"I have no riddles for you," I said, "but I do have a question. It's bothered me since we spoke. Why didn't you just come and talk to me once you learned what I was? Why orchestrate the metamorphic night?"

He shrugged. "It was a question of scale. I needed an illustration of your capabilities. And you needed to understand exactly who and what I am before we talked. That way I would have your undivided attention."

"In other words, you're even crazier than I thought."

He tapped a finger so hard against his skull I could hear it. "Think about it, moon kitten, you would never have believed a word I said if I had not proved Magistrate Winter's deceit."

"Did you do that? I don't think you proved anything."

He vanished within a puff of blue smoke. When he reappeared, he was standing inches from me. I tried to step away, but he was too quick. He grabbed my wrists and pulled me closer. I fought but he gripped tighter.

An arm folded around my waist, his other hand interlocked fingers with mine, and away we went, spinning and twisting in a painful, bizarre, old-fashioned sort of dance.

"Let yourself go, Luna Mae," he said. "You're as brittle and stiff as a dried-up old witch. You must live a little while you live forever."

He kept spinning me, his eyes hooked onto mine, and I gave up trying to control anything. I let him lead, curious as to where this was going, and soon enough we were waltzing to a phantom tune, kicking aside debris and broken glass with our dancing feet.

The lunatic smelled good. I detected lavender and clove. His dark hair fell to his shoulders—vitality shone through his eyes.

After a while, he loosened his hold and I pushed him away.

"Don't be a stick-in-the-mud, jellybean," he said, pouting. "Dance with me more before the day is lost."

I planted my hands on my waist. "No."

He reached out his hand and I slapped it away.

"What part of *no* don't you understand?"

His mouth bent into an impish smirk. "A word of such finality means nothing to those of us who shall never end."

I walked away, snarling under my breath. I felt his gaze on my backside and turned around. I caught his eyes on me for a fraction of a second before he looked away.

I glanced down to scan my own body. I had on a plaid pleated skirt and a white bell sleeve top, both of which accentuated my figure.

"Are you checking out my butt?" I asked Chaos. "Haven't you seen enough of them over the centuries?"

"Have you seen enough sunsets? Listened to enough Mozart? Eaten enough crème brûlée?"

Point taken.

He got suddenly serious. "But no, I wasn't checking out your gluteus maximus muscles. I would never be so tactless."

"Why? Something wrong with them?"

For the first time he pondered his answer. "It is against code."

"You have a code? Now I know you're full of shit."

"You're a mist rider," he said, solemnly.

I had to admit, he almost had me convinced.

"Then why were you staring?"

He looked down, thinking. "The way you ambulate is reminiscent of someone I once knew. It's uncanny."

I rolled my eyes. "*Ambulate?* You actually expect me to believe that."

"Yes," he said, absentmindedly. "You have the same walk. You even pivot the same, your arms swing the same."

Seeing Chaos contemplate with those savage eyes was as disorientating as if watching a bull sit down for a cup of tea.

"Enough nonsense," I said. "Where's the proof you promised?"

"Right," he said and headed for the kitchen.

The mad Immortal rummaged through shattered glass and discarded piles of plates, bowls and mugs, the whole time humming a tune that sounded like the Russian national anthem.

I had given up trying to understand what went through that lunatic's head, but this was a whole other level of unstable.

"You think the proof lies there among my broken china?"

He stood up, holding a large oval platter with handles. "This will do," he said, placing it on the coffee table.

Chaos walked to the window, whistling, and bent over the ledge to find a cord hanging down from the window. Once gathered, he found a brown plastic bag at the end of the cord.

He shook the bag over the coffee table. A head rolled out and onto the platter with a thud. It was in grotesque condition—bald, skin the color of ash, small eyes like buttonholes peering at me, a nose so flat it looked like someone had glued two nostrils in the middle of a face and a long blue tongue sticking out of its mouth. Yet, this head appeared to have once belonged to a human.

I took a step back. "What the hell is that? Are you completely fucking mental? Forget it. Just tell me, who did you kill?"

He dismissed my questioning with a wave of his hand. "The creature's past is of no importance. Pay attention to what it has to say now."

"What do you mean *what it has to say*? It's an inanimate skull. Wait, do you think it talks to you? Oh shit, I have to get out of here."

I clamped my mouth shut when steam started pouring out of the head's fucking eyes, ears and nostrils as if its brain was boiling inside.

Chaos held his hand above the head, palm down. The head jerked forward on the platter. Chaos closed his fist. The eyes fluttered; a viscous liquid poured out of the mouth.

"That's necromancy," I said, taken aback.

He smirked. "What can I say? Being a Shadow comes with certain perks."

"I want nothing to do with this," I insisted.

He clutched my hand and held it tight. Magic boiled inside my veins, willing me to strike down this psycho about to chat with a severed head in my home. The offense was so staggering I couldn't fathom it. Necromancy was strictly forbidden in all supernatural and paranormal circles. If it was detected coming out of my home, I would be banished and shamed, never allowed to practice magic or communicate with my peers or even my family.

"You worry too much, chipmunk," Chaos said, reading my mind. "What happens in Sophie's apartment stays in Sophie's apartment. It's our secret. Your paltry witchery orbs and your anemic telepathic factions cannot pierce through my utter domination of etheric fields."

I reeled in my elemental energy and took a deep breath. I knew he had the power to contain whatever magic he performed tonight and prevent the orbs from registering the slightest reverberation. I still felt queasy even witnessing such dark and sadistic arts.

Chaos clapped his free hand on his thigh. The head levitated above the platter, quaking and grinding its teeth. If it weren't him holding my hand, I would have fled.

The dried-out eyes grew wet, the bony nose widened, and its tongue turned purply red. The face took on a blush as it formed a shocked expression.

"Show me how you died, you fiend," Chaos ordered the head, his voice commanding and deep like a subterranean rumble.

The head's eyes darkened, the white in them vanishing, and a mist cone projected out of them to form a hologram. In it, I saw what I knew to be one of the Seventh Council's underground courts. A man came forward—completely hairless, severe-looking, with sparkling bronze skin, a folded papyrus in his right hand. Magistrate Argos.

A shorter man entered the space inside the hologram and bowed. He was bald with bluish skin and a long scarlet cape. In his small, buttonhole eyes I recognized the dead head.

Argos handed the man the papyrus and a thin, silver ice snake. My skin prickled. Ice snakes, or Shaervas as they were called in the elder scrolls, were instruments for clandestine witchcraft that could adulterate magic sources, infusing them with dark energy. When combined with wicked spells, they could infiltrate the Deep Down itself.

The short man, whose head now projected homemade movies in my living room, made a curtsy and left.

The scene changed. My stomach lunged into my mouth. The man was standing outside a Deep Down portal, papyrus unfolded in his right hand, Shaerva at his feet, his lips working at a spell.

Chaos showed up behind him like an angel of death, hood covering his head, his enormous Damascus blade raised. He beheaded the man the second he turned to face him, then chopped Shaerva into quarters.

The hologram faded, the head fell to the platter and Chaos released my hand. There was visible fatigue on his features. So, his power was not inexhaustible. Necromancy must have taken a toll on anyone. I filed that observation away, then finally exhaled heavily after what I had witnessed.

Chaos reached inside his coat and pulled out the papyrus. My worst fears were realized. An ancient spell was written inside, a malicious curse meant to bypass the wards of the

Deep Down and install corrosive magic.

"The creature was shielded with Immortal essence that made it invisible to your kind's magic and to the Deep Down tech," he said. "But not to papa Chaos," he added in a proud, sing-song voice.

"Are you expecting me to be grateful? You thwarted Argos. Great, but you cannot possibly expect me to believe you don't have your own agenda here."

He grinned, completely satisfied, and without a word walked to the window and swung his leg out, saddling the windowsill like a horse.

"That's it?" I said. "Just a skull movie and no more explanation?"

"I gave you your proof about the Seventh, but I wouldn't share any of this to the good magistrate, buttercup," he said, looking me over. "If he opts to come after me, I will kill him this time. My generosity has limits."

Against my better judgment, I went for defiance. "I didn't need your proof. I already knew about Düsternis and his plans."

He could not have been more thrilled. His head fell back, his eyes shut, and he chuckled silently. "You are precious! You went to Magistrate Winter with my information? Oh, how I would have delighted in seeing his face."

Before I could respond, blue smoke came for Chaos and he was gone.

With every answer he had provided, another three, four,

five new questions arose. And what about that creepy, weird dance?

What the hell was that, Chaos? You total freak.

Chapter 14

Fresh snow packed the majestic slope. Scattered trees were all dressed up in the fluffy white fashion of the Yukon. I rubbed my gloved hands together and marveled at snowflakes dancing their way onto a landscape of complete stillness.

My breath came to life in vaporized puffs that lingered in the air before I blew them away.

I looked back to see Whitehorse in the distance. The quaint town lay down in a quiet basin, with specks of white roofs amongst Lodgepole pines, spruce and fir trees.

"How much longer?" I asked Winter who walked ahead.

He turned back. "If you are cold, I can warm you."

"I'm good, thanks. I just want to get to Emmet and set him free."

Winter considered the path before us. "We're less than a

mile out." He furrowed his brow. "I thought we'd be able to see the facility by now."

"Are we lost?"

He plodded on, refusing to dignify my question with an answer. I trudged after him.

The Yukon River glistened about a hundred yards to the west, frozen across its banks. The mere sight of it made my bones shiver.

Behind a thick line of fir trees, a dome of ice emerged ahead like a gigantic igloo.

"There," Winter said, picking up speed. "The holding facility lies beneath the dome."

My heart raced as fear and anticipation mixed into an adrenaline cocktail. It was well and good to remain positive and assume our info was correct and we'd soon be rescuing Emmet, but it was just as likely we'd be ambushed, or that Emmet would be seriously injured—or worse.

When we reached the dome, Winter circled around, looking for a way in.

"Where's the door?" I asked. Apparently, I was Miss Obvious today.

He shot me a dismissive look. "I'm trying to find it."

I studied the dome up close. It was about fifteen feet tall and maybe twenty feet wide. There were no cracks, no lines, no scratches, no markings of any sort that I could see. Just uniform, bluish-white frost.

Winter took off his leather gloves to feel the icy surface. He slid his hand around the dome, his fingers searching for signs of partitions.

He walked back next to me and rubbed his hands. His eyes never left the igloo. A low, rumbling sound came from below ground. Chunks of ice cracked and slipped from the dome like falling dominoes. It was as if a giant hand was flaying the frost with an ice pick.

What was left, was a new layer of solid ice. There was no indication that this layer was any more penetrable than the layer that had just fallen away.

Winter clenched his teeth. A tangle of blue energy fields glowed bright in his right hand. He shook his arm and the hissing blazes leapt forward, dividing into separate lines that struck the dome from different angles.

Wow! Now that was some next level magic. I'd need a full moon to even attempt anything like that.

The ice sizzled as it took the blasts, the shafts of energy slashing and digging deep into the frost.

Chilling doubts settled into my bones. I shivered. There would be nothing here except a dome of pure ice and more ice.

"Are you going to help or what?" Winter said. His aura had turned a dark purple, the color of anger.

"What would be the point? I can't match your power, not out here in the middle of this polar landscape. Freezing temperatures weaken elemental energy even when it's made from water. You'll be done before I could muster up much energy at all. I mean, your name's freaking Winter."

It was true. In theory, I could melt the ice to use the water's elemental energy, but there was only so much you could extract from frozen elements.

His piercing blue eyes stared at me. "When will you get it into your head that you don't need the elements to draw out your power? You're a lunar witch only by training, Luna. It's time to accept that you're a mist rider. All the magic sources in all the realms are at your disposal."

I frowned. "Fine, but I sense no sources right now."

"There is a ley line intersection to the east, merely a mile from here. Use that, tap into it, and start acting like the prodigy of magic that you are."

"Come on, Jonas, only electrokinetics and a few master sorcerers can tap into ley lines and control that kind of power."

"You are every kind of magic if you only will it, Luna Mae," he said, exasperated. "At very least, you could give the old college try."

It sounded nice but... a ley line was the most volatile and abundant source of magic outside the Deep Down. They were hyper-charmed currents overflowing with accessible energy. Unlike the Deep Down, where magic was natural and an impossible to resist instinct for all supernatural creatures, ley line energy had to be extracted delicately and handled expertly.

Or else... *kaboom!*

I closed my eyes and measured my breathing. Locating the ley line intersection could only be accomplished if I retook control of my vitals which were now completely under assault from the frigid environment.

It took me a few minutes to slow my pulse and lock onto its location. Once engaged, it felt like riding a tidal wave, pulling in moisture until it built up to an astounding magnitude. I had never felt anything like it—it was overriding my control.

My body strained as I tried to blend the ley line energy into my usual current of elemental magic, but my failure was about to combust and become a problem on a nuclear scale if not for Winter.

His energy had augmented exponentially, having tapped into the ley line while I was struggling to get a grip of it. I sensed his power gnaw into my etheric field as it exploded, splitting the ice dome in half.

The last vestiges of hope died with a thud as the two halves collapsed onto a solid ice base. My insides frosted... every bit of my core ached.

"What if Emmet had been inside?" I yelled.

But he wasn't. We had come out here for nothing. I'd bought thermals and snow pants and a puffy white jacket that made me look like the Michelin Man for nothing. We'd been fed fake intel again. Great. We had been supernaturally trolled. Or worse, we were out here doing dirty work for an evil entity.

Winter growled, then instantly recomposed himself. He started back to Whitehorse, saying nothing. I opened my mouth to scream but never did. By the time we got back to the hotel, the sky had turned a dark mauve.

He bolted up the stairs, climbing three steps at a time, and exploded through our room's door. He tossed aside his jacket and kicked off his boots. The room was large and rustic. The floor and the paneled walls were all knotted wood planks. He knelt in front of the fireplace to get a fire going.

I hung up my puffy jacket, then plugged in the tiny Christmas tree on the mantel top. I dropped into one of the two armchairs facing the fireplace to remove my boots and snow pants.

Winter stacked logs onto the tinder and then struck a wooden match. It took a few seconds to get a spark that would grow into a fire.

Rising to his feet, he stood directly over me. He was devoid of all emotions, even confidence. The weary Immortal had never looked so human. There was a sense he could feel all those many thousands of years now like an unwanted weight he wanted to flee.

The fire light danced and sparkled in his gaze.

"I'll run another check in the database," he said. "I am unlikely to find anything, but I need to stay busy."

I knew what he meant. He had to keep his *from-another-time* rage under control, which must be difficult after millennia in a warrior clan.

He flipped the laptop open on the bed and logged onto the hotel's wi-fi.

My cringy flip phone buzzed. Lucia had texted.

As I read her words, I started to feel like I was suffocating.

I placed my hand on Winter's shoulder. "You have to see this."

He took the phone and read the screen.

> *The wolf was moved. Now at the Sacred Vault of the Brooks Range.*

Dark shadows loomed inside Winter's eyes. "How does your friend's mom possess such knowledge? How does she even know about the missing wolf?"

My goose is cooked.

"Don't look at me. I didn't tell her anything."

Winter arched an eyebrow. "That narrows it down to one."

Chaos. Which meant he was either the one pulling the strings the whole time, or he had already figured everything out. He told me he would.

"He has given us a clue on how to find him," Winter went on. "Which can mean only one thing. He wants to be found."

"Well…"

Winter glared at me. "Luna, no! Please, tell me I'm wrong."

"I might have tipped him off."

His savage glare made it damn near impossible to hold his stare.

"He came to the apartment," I explained.

"You never learn. When?"

I tried to gulp non-existent saliva. "Last night. He brought me what he called evidence of Düsternis's plot to wreak havoc on the Deep Down. I told him I knew everything already."

"What proof did he give you?"

Right. That part.

"A head... a talking head, well, no, a little projector head, like a real decomposing head that was also a projector." I had to stop to regather my focus. "So, this thing created a hologram and inside that I saw Argos. He was dispatching a corrosive spell along with a silver Shaerva to the head... the man who once had the head, you know, on his shoulders. The spell was meant to infiltrate a Deep Down portal. Chaos asked me not to tell you."

"And how did the man lose his head?" Winter said with a tone that told me he had already guessed.

"Your old chum did what you guys do," I said. "That evil *slashity* slash off with their head thing."

My crazy words had little effect on him. This man must have seen it all during his long life not to react to such outlandish tales.

"Let's summarize," he said. "Immediately after we barely kept our cover on a wild goose chase in Tijuana, and while I'm on this mission specifically as a personal favor to you, Chaos, our number one suspect, paid you a visit and performed necromancy in the privacy of your home. Then, he somehow convinced you to lie to me and you obliged, deliberately leaving me in the dark, despite the possible risk to, *well*, everything. How am I doing?"

I really didn't want to answer. "In what sense?" I finally said.

He breathed heavily. His chest expanded and contracted as he stewed on the whole scenario. "There's no sense. None, Luna. At some point, you have to decide who you trust."

"I didn't want you to go after Chaos," I said. "I know that's what he wanted. Jonas, he wanted to have a reason to kill you. And now you'll just go confront him and he'll get his wish. That's why I didn't tell you."

"That's my choice, not yours." He sighed. "Your choice is, which side are you going to be on?"

There it was again. *Sides.* Celia's prophecy haunting my every step.

"Okay, I should have come to you, obviously, but now we're on the same page and we have to do something. According to Chaos, the Düsternis plan is very much alive and kicking. The Council is moving ahead at full speed. There will be no reprieve, no postponement."

I knew those words would sting. Düsternis had kept Winter in the dark, most likely because Winter had lost the Grand Magistrate's trust.

He slapped his thigh and got up. "Pack your things. We're going back. We must check on Lucia, see that she is well and see what Chaos has done to her and with her and see what, if anything, she knows."

Did he truly care about Lucia's health and well-being?

"It could be a trap," I said.

"The Sacred Vault or checking on Lucia?" he said with a grin.

"Either. Both."

He laughed. "Now we're on the same page."

I started to pack up my things, quickly. I tried to remember everything I knew about the Sacred Vault. It was an ancient Immortal archive, but this archive was often mentioned in the darkest of tales of pre-history. Mere mention of it gave chills to all. There were details there on the lives of every Immortal and Eternal that ever existed; they were buried in rickety catacombs deep below the northernmost peak of the Brooks Range in Northern Alaska.

"Does this implicate the Seventh Council in Emmet's abduction?" I said.

He never answered. Of course not, but I had begun to know Winter. I knew that whenever he didn't answer, the answer was always *yes*, and that meant the Seventh Council may well have taken my ex-boyfriend.

I knew also that Winter cared about my well-being and Lucia's, too.

In the car to the airport the darkness crept in from all sides, and I could feel Chaos watching—his black eyes were always out there, watching, like the stars, like the moon.

No, he wasn't there in Whitehorse. I wasn't losing my mind, but Chaos knew our every move long before we did.

Chapter 15

We headed straight for Lucia's from the airport after a wild ride on the freeway in Winter's old Civic. When we arrived, it was just past seven in the evening.

Winter banged on the door repeatedly before I took hold of his hand to stop him. Frustrated with his vexed attitude, I rang the doorbell, as if that simple gesture could calm his aggression.

It took Lucia two minutes to come to the door. She wore a lacy burgundy nightgown with spaghetti straps and side slits. I stared at her a long while, quite stunned to see her in a sexy nightgown at 7:10 pm.

"Sophie, Jonas," she said, brushing back her long, dark curls. "Well, that's a surprise. Lily's on campus tonight."

"Good," Winter said and strolled past Lucia and into the house.

"I'm sorry to just show up," I said, finding my voice. "Can we come in?"

She raised an eyebrow. "One of you already has."

Lucia closed the door after I stepped inside. Her eyes followed my every move as I found Winter in the living room pacing back and forth.

"Is everything okay?" she said.

"You're dressed quite sensually," Winter said. "Perhaps you've had a visit from a gentleman caller wanting to use your telepathic channel?"

Lucia's eyes widened. "I beg your pardon!"

I glared at Winter. "Never mind him. He's had a long trip. Lucia, you sent me a text last night, a cryptic text, hard to interpret."

Lucia raised her hands, dumbfounded. "I didn't send any texts to you, Sophie, or to anyone. Now, I really don't know what this is all about, but tomorrow would be a better day for it. I am in the middle of something."

She marched to the front door. Winter stepped in her way and placed both hands on her shoulders. "Stay still," he said.

Lucia tried to break free, but he quickly subdued her. I saw the struggle in her eyes. It made me feel sick to my stomach.

"Sophie, I warned you about this man. He is possessive and brutish."

Well, that is hard to argue.

Winter moved his hands onto her temples and pressed. His jaw tightened and his eyes narrowed.

Lucia yelped.

Shaking off my stupor, I physically removed his hands from her temples.

"That's enough." I knew he had allowed me to remove his hands. I couldn't have done it otherwise.

Lucia was shaking, completely freaked out. I believed it was sincere.

"A word," Winter said through clenched teeth.

He ushered me to the back of the room.

"She has no clue what we're talking about," I said. "Don't you think Chaos would have wiped her memory again?"

He shook his head. "There's no change in the connective path. It's undisturbed. No recent activity at all. He hasn't used her."

"What's going on then? What about the text?"

A male voice boomed from another room. "What's all the hubbub, honeybee? Have the Mormons invaded the living room?"

Chaos sauntered into the room in nothing but red boxer briefs. His build was more like body armor than flesh, all sinewy, corded muscle, and tanned, hairless skin. He had the same double-headed eagle tattoo as Winter inked across his chest, but his was less golden and more bronze.

He fussed with a paper rabbit in his hands, folding the paper edges with precise care. "Who and what has the cat dragged in?"

"My daughter's friend," Lucia said, still rattled.

Chaos took her in his arms and pet her hair back. "Forgive us," he said. "You have caught us ill-disposed."

"Sophie, this is a friend," Lucia said, blushing. "Zack Wisdom."

Wisdom! You've got to be kidding me.

"As I said, now is not a good time," she went on.

"And the big fella," Chaos said. "Does he have a name?"

"That's Jonas. He was just going," Lucia said with venom.

"Nonsense," Chaos said. "Don't run them off on my account, Lucy Lue. I'm beginning to feel rather chatty."

The moment Chaos let go of Lucia, Winter needed all of two seconds to get his fellow Shadow into a headlock.

Lucia gasped and covered her mouth. I put my arm around her.

"They're old friends," I said to assure her. "Army buddies."

Chaos chuckled, holding onto Winter's arm around his throat. "Not bad, golden boy."

"Jonas, that's quite enough," I said. "Don't let him get under your skin."

Winter released the headlock, yanking Chaos forward.

Chaos laughed. "Well, someone likes it rough."

That just about does it.

"You think this is funny?" I yelled at Chaos. "What did you do with Emmet, you son of a bitch? I can see what you've done with Lucia."

Chaos winked. "Consenting adults."

He reached out to touch Lucia's forehead. She froze on the spot, like she had been lobotomized. She stood rigid like a statue. An immobilizing spell affected both her mind and body.

"Better to let the busy little bee rest," Chaos said.

Stirring energy clenched my insides, wanting to strike out and crush his skull. I resisted the impulse for a few seconds when a thin beam of energy escaped my control. I directed the sweltering whip at the center of his bare abdomen. It slashed through his skin like a propane torch, opening a sizzling hole the size of a penny, burning its way into his stomach.

I had hit him with so much power my hands tingled.

Chaos gasped. His eyes locked on mine. "Is that all you got?"

Feel the burn, you evil bastard.

"What did you do to Lucia?" I asked.

"The thing I like most about you, sugar pop... you're impetuous, you err on the side of defiance every time like all charming simpletons."

I squeezed the energy that poured out of my fingers, tightening it like a vise, sharpening the edges to lodge them deep inside his flesh like tiny hooks. Yeah, I had no illusions that he could easily defeat me, or at least block my magic, but with Winter there, Chaos might think twice about unleashing his power against both of us.

In a blink my sizzling hooks were buried up and down his abdomen.

Chaos winced. His voice came out strained but determined. "Fine, I don't like to kiss and tell, but I just sexed the hell out of the little busy bee, gave her the best o's of her life, doubt she ever came close to having six, no, wait, seven in a row, so you see, I've been generous and shown enormous restraint. I even listened to her whining about her work situation—did you know they moved her language class to the science building and then cancelled the annual Latin poetry reading? Sadly, I do. And I let her live after that. It wasn't easy. It would have been justified homicide. She nearly killed me with boredom."

"Were you ever funny?" I said. "Like maybe a thousand years ago? I'm curious. Truly."

He chuckled like a maniac. "No worries here, my little mean girl. For all your replacement Mommy figure knows, it's the first time we've met. I texted you when she was in the shower. Easy peasy." He pouted. "I did not connect to her telepathic channel. I am sure Frosty here already told you that. I gave you my word, pumpkin, remember?"

I released him. Maybe I had just signed my death warrant. Would he ever let go of this moment when I humiliated him in front of his archrival? Or would he wait patiently for this to be done and finally kill me?

"All right," I said. "So, you wanted our attention. Here we are."

Chaos pointed at Winter. "Not him. Just you. Ask grumpy to wait outside."

Winter crossed his thick arms on his chest. He wasn't going anywhere.

"Winter stays," I said.

"Uh-uh," Chaos said. "That won't work for me. His temper is a detriment to an open dialogue. He might lose his marbles and go for my head and I don't want a rerun where I'm about to chop him to pieces and you crack open the Earth to save your pathetic mentor. I mean, why ruin Lucia's charming little house, eh, sugar donut?"

Having no desire to prove Chaos wrong, Winter immediately lost it. When I saw his eyes smoldering, I leaped in front of him. He pushed past me like I was a fly and lunged at Chaos, landing a kick to his solar plexus, knocking the breath out of Chaos who smashed back against the wall.

Chaos rebounded right off the wall and slammed into Winter. I had to jump aside to avoid being trampled.

I had enough. I spun around and used a gravitational force to freeze a chair in midflight before it went through the window.

Wow, I've never done that before.

The two Shadow Warriors engaged in hand-to-hand combat and even as they strained to the point where the muscles and veins in their necks looked like they might burst, I knew they were holding back, I knew they were just letting off some steam.

Maybe I should dispose of them both now while they were busy with each other. Surely, mist riders had ways to deal with misbehaving Immortals.

Instead of killing them, I wrapped them both in a shimmering lasso of energy. I yelled. "Have you gotten it out of your systems yet?"

Lucia remained petrified, like her spirit had left her body. She wouldn't remember any of this, but at what cost to her mind?

"Winter, please, let me talk to the psycho. We don't have time to waste."

The two men pushed apart. Winter growled. "After you finish with this nonsense, he's mine. I will not let eternity be cursed with this trash."

Chaos laughed. "Goals are good, brother. Delusions are not."

Winter cursed under his breath in a language I did not understand, then slammed the door behind him.

Chaos tilted his head. "He's a total bore, eh?"

His stomach had healed, only a pink dot remained as evidence of the deep wound I had given him. A cut above his lip vanished right in front of my eyes, and a purple bruise stopped spreading across his pecs and turned a yellowish green. I sighed. My life had become The Twilight Zone.

"Please, put some clothes on," I said.

"Clothes, such tedium!"

He went to the bedroom and came back wearing a gray

crew neck workout shirt and black mesh running shorts.

I arched an eyebrow. Why did Lucia fall for this guy every time he showed up? They couldn't possibly have shared interests. Was sex the only thing she was looking for in a man?

"Do you ever wear anything other than black or gray?" I asked.

He shrugged. "I find bright colors unappealing. The old world was more to my tastes. Animal skins and necklaces made of teeth. *Muah! Favolosa!*"

Right. "I'm going to give you this chance to come clean and tell me about your text, or I'll call Winter in and I'll be his backup. You might think that you're a badass, but I'd like to see you fight both of us."

I amused him. "Prickly little rabbit, has your thickskulled mentor not taught you a thing? No one can come between two shadow warriors when they are fighting to the death."

"I'm not sure your Immortal traditions and rules apply to mist riders and I'm willing to bet you're not sure either. Anyway, I'm game. Bring it on, Chaos. Wait, you weren't so cocky earlier when I sliced you up with my fire whip. You would have blocked a witch's magic effortlessly, but *my* magic? Hmmm."

What was I doing? I needed to get him to talk, not slash my throat.

He licked his lips. "Senseless child. You won't see many more winters." He chuckled. "See what I did there?"

I sat on the couch and crossed my legs. "I'm waiting. You

wouldn't have sent that text if you didn't want to have a chat."

He squatted in front of me to look me straight in the eye. "Sometimes, I feel like we've met, wee girl, long ago. Yes, fine, the chat. Fair enough. It has begun. The Eternal portals have opened. Heinous creatures long exiled have reentered the world. I would guess their moods to be rather foul."

This confirmed Winter's interpretation of Seventh Council data about the exile vortex, but I chose to act indifferent. "What are you on about?"

"I mean, the Deep Down is in deep shit." He inhaled as if losing interest. "Your brood, the charmed folk, are about to get pummeled."

"What's this got to do with Emmet? You're stalling."

"Must I spell it out for you? The Immortal who has the wolf in the Sacred Vault works with those responsible for opening the gates of hell."

"The portals?"

"Why yes, kitty cat," he said. "Did you really not know from where the concept of hell was born?"

"I don't get it. How does it all connect?"

"I'll go slowly," Chaos said, literally talking slowly. "Someone up in the Eternal Halls doesn't like you. They don't trust you. They recruited that fuckstick Düsternis to investigate. Making sense now?"

"That may be your theory, or maybe my theory is true. Want to hear it?"

"Do I?"

"I think you do," I told him. "My theory goes like this. You are behind the whole thing and you're lying through your teeth."

"Yowzers, it's like I'm talking to a wall. Run along and tell your impulsive beefcake manfriend what I've told you. See what he tells you. At very least the self-serving bastard can see through elaborate schemes. You, however, *yikes*. You are a staggering waste of potential, sadly, a slow-learning infant."

If looks could kill, he'd be dead. "And you learned this how?"

"Oh, bother. Not important. The way I see it, you have two choices: you can be off to the Sacred Vault before the 8 o'clock chimes, or you can wait until they're ready for you and toss you more crumbs. That way you can walk right into their trap. Best go now and steal the wolf from under their noses."

"Oh, right, because it's that simple."

"Listen carefully, Luna. You're running out of time. Tell me, what is your connection with this Groshek creature? Lovers? Cause you can do better."

Was that an offer? Ew.

"None of your business."

"How can I effectively advise you without trust?"

Did he say trust? "Okay, buddy, if you're so certain, then why don't you just come along and help me save Emmet?"

"Me? You don't want to be my partner, remember?"

"Huh," I gloated. "You see, you're all bark and no bite."

His face contorted. "If you want my help, you'd have to sign on for my battle against the Immortal Councils."

"Yeah, hard pass."

"At loggerheads, yet again. More's the pity. Do try not to lose your pretty little head before we meet again."

He was about to go up in blue smoke when I remembered Lucia.

"Dude, your girlfriend!"

"Ah," he said. "Sweet Lucia. Yes. You know, before you accuse me again of having no bite, you might want to behold this lovely lady's bum."

"Gross, jackass!"

He readied his finger to bring her back.

"Chaos, wait. What is the danger approaching the Deep Down? Can you at least make sure they stay safe?"

He raised an eyebrow. "What's in it for me?"

Give me patience!

"A hearty meal for your ego. I know you'd love to save the world."

"The world as in the *basic* world. That's where I have vested interests. The Deep Down? Not so much. It's like Cleveland. I could make do without."

"Ah, I know guys like you. Big talkers, but they never lift a finger."

"You think I want to be a hero? To whom? Witches? Basics? I was not raised in the era of chivalry, sugarplum.

Martyrdom, the savior complex? Those are the pseudo-psycho derangements of your time, not mine."

"Do your thing with Lucia," I reminded him.

"Already have done," he said with a wink. "She'll be fine."

"You are such a creepy old man," I said. "Don't ever go near her again, under any circumstances, do I make myself clear?"

He started spinning, slowly at first with arms outstretched, then faster, like a child trying to get dizzy. "Blah, blah, blah… here comes the fun police!"

Blue smoke snaked up his legs.

I grabbed his arm. "This isn't the end."

Chaos locked two feral eyes on mine. "I already know how it ends, baby witch rider, and so do you!"

His arm shrunk away from my grip and he was gone.

Lucia gasped. I turned to take her hand and steady her.

"Sophie," she said, blinking three times. "When did you get here?"

I smiled, relieved. "I was just looking for Lil."

She squinted her eyes to remember. "Lily's on campus tonight."

"Yes," I said. "You were telling me that when you got faint."

"Oh, dear," she said, still trying to remember.

"It's okay, I caught you."

"You're a good girl. So lovely. And the only friend of Lil's I like."

"Thanks," I said. "I think you need to lie down. I'll help you."

She nodded, then noticed her sexy nightgown. "Oh, Sophie, what in the world am I wearing?"

"It's flattering," I said, leading her to the bedroom.

"Well, I do try to stay fit," Lucia said, beaming. "You never quite know when you'll meet an interesting man."

Chapter 16

WINTER DROVE AWAY AS soon as he dropped me off. He said he'd go see what he could find about the Sacred Vault—if anything. His expression on our way back to his condo had been blank, his body language unreadable. I had no idea whether he thought Chaos's story was credible or not.

Gaining access to the vault archives wouldn't be easy, he'd said. Nobody was allowed entrance without special authorization from the highest officials. If Chaos was right about Emmet, just filing the petition might raise red flags with the Seventh Council and beyond.

I barely slept that night. I got up at sunrise and sat by the window in Winter's living room, feeling drained and restless at the same time, mulling over the conversation with Chaos in my head.

A light breeze blew through the half-open window, in-fusing me with some much-needed energy, when the phone rang. It was Faion.

"Hey," I said, "everything alright?"

"How fast can we get to Palomar Mountain?"

"That's like two hours away, Faion."

There was a gate to the Deep Down in the forested area of the State Park on Palomar Mountain. Not a coincidence, I suspected.

Faion snickered. *"One and a half tops."*

"You're forgetting the walking part to the gate."

"Damn," he said. *"Math."*

I needed his humor. "What's going on, Faion?"

"It's another Gran thing. You know your friend, Tam? Turns out she knows my gran and my gran wants us to meet with Tam, both of us."

"And we're meeting at the gate on Palomar Mountain?"

"Thought I said that. Get your bony buns moving."

I closed the window and grabbed my jacket. "Okay, I'm coming."

The Uber driver pulled up to Faion who was pacing in front of his dorm. We barely talked during the ride. The Uber driver didn't need to hear about shifters and shadows and for sure not soul swallowers.

Palomar Mountain State Park had a beautiful forest com-plete with long and winding hiking trails, scattered fishing ponds and large campsites. I had been there a few times.

I could almost smell the pine and fir and cedar trees as we drove.

A gigantic incense cedar served as the Palomar gate to the Deep Down. Nearly 200 feet tall and with a trunk over ten feet in diameter, it was hard to miss.

The orange brown bark on the trunk was weathered and fissured and ready to disintegrate. At first look, it didn't look like the tree held any special significance. To most it was just an anonymous old tree on the mountain. To those of us who knew a certain spell that could split the bottom part of the trunk in two, it was a gateway to a hidden world of wonders.

Once open, two hundred steps led you down to a circular chamber with multiple transition portals, each one of which could instantly transport you to different gateways of the West Coast underground network.

In a sense, the Palomar gateway was the mother of all gateways.

A bowstring snapped. An arrow stuck in the ground at our feet.

Faion backed away while I stepped in front to protect him. We both looked up to find Tam sitting on a tree branch, clutching her bow and grinning from ear to ear.

"You should have seen your faces," she said, laughing. "Faion, I'm sorry if I caused you to defecate. There are leaves everywhere if you need them."

"You a nasty girl," Faion said. "That's what you are."

Tam hopped down and straightened her arms over

her head to stretch.

"We came as fast as we could," I said.

"Next time come as fast as *I* can," she said. "I was starting to develop a bad case of kyphosis hunched up there."

"Why were you waiting on top of the tree portal?" I said.

"I'm not supposed to be here," she said, "but Celia insisted I get you up to speed on the latest developments."

She led the way through the forest until we came to a narrow stream. We crossed it and approached another huge incense cedar. We sat at its feet. Tam offered us her water canteen. The ground was cold and wet.

"What's this my gran wants us to know?" Faion said.

Tam's gaze intensified. "A troglodyte convoy has visited the Deep Down to discuss matters with Horpheus, Helianna and the rest of the Board of Supernatural Orders. They have disclosed that part of their elite fighting force under a General Orsenio have broken away to form an alliance with wielders of dark magic. The convoy has offered to assist us. They recommend barricading our communities and bracing for the coming storm."

"The Deep Down is the alliance's target?" Faion said.

"They said we needed to act fast or get caught in the crossfire." Tam glanced my way and lowered her voice. "There have been reverberations in the orbs, like someone's checking our defenses."

Argos and his Shaervas no doubt.

I decided to test the waters, see how much Tam knew.

"The troglodytes don't have the kind of magic that would be required for such a task. Did they mention who's behind the dark alliance?"

She shook her head. "I don't know. What we do know is that there are necromancers involved as well as several old exiled mages and sorcerers, but Celia didn't say if the troglodyte convoy have revealed who's pulling the strings—it's possible they don't have that information themselves."

I glanced at Faion. He nodded, giving me his blessing.

"Tam, there is so much that you don't know. The Eternal Gates have been opened and the exile vortex has been compromised."

"That's not possible," she said.

"It's true, I'm afraid, but that's not the worst part. The Seventh Council has plans to unleash war on all magic and supernatural factions, starting with the Deep Down. They have extremely potent Immortals among them who can control and convert elemental and other Earth energy. Even a few Eternals are on their side."

"Holy shit," Tam said.

"That's not all," I continued. "They can exert absolute control over human technology. Their ultimate design is to make the entire planet grovel at their feet so they can assume dominion over everything and everyone still alive."

Tam stared at me, flabbergasted.

"What she said," Faion added.

"As crazy as this sounds, we have allies among the Immortals," I said to cushion the blow. "If it comes to that, the Deep Down won't be alone, not completely anyway."

"Yeah," Faion said, "just extremely outgunned."

Tam considered my words. "Luna, this sounds like crazy talk."

"That's because it's completely bonkers," I agreed.

"Yeah," Tam said.

"Yeah," Faion said.

"Listen, Tam," I said, putting my hand on her shoulder. "Tell Celia about all this, she'll know what to do next."

Tam nodded, trying to make sense of it all. "I will."

I rose. Faion did, too. "We really have to go."

Tam climbed to her feet. She looked to Faion. They had a moment.

Faion stepped in front of me. "I'm needed here, Luna. This is my home. I need to be with Gran and this message needs to be delivered by someone who can convince her of its certainty."

I also needed Faion. It was starting to feel like a lonely world, but I didn't have a second to spare. Winter could be back with his approved petition at any moment and we'd have to get on a plane.

"Yeah, okay," I said. "I guess, yeah. This is your home. Make sure Celia believes all of it. That's right. You're right. Go."

Faion had trained all his life for a moment like this when

his charisma could help protect his own. He had grown so much since the day we met.

I took Tam's hand in mine. "Faion is of one mind with me. What I know, he knows. His skills and courage will be great assets to you."

"I will protect him," Tam said. "Him and all who dwell here."

Tears threatened as I hugged my friends tight, wishing I could stay by their side and fight, wishing to reveal the truth of my origins and my destiny.

Nobody except Winter and Chaos knew I was a mist rider and I had to keep it that way long enough to come upon a mist horse. It might be our best and only chance to tip the scales of what was to come.

Leaving Tam and Faion behind, I started to run and then I ran faster and faster until the wind dried my eyes.

Chapter 17

IT WAS HALF PAST six and already dark when Winter returned. He looked like a man who hadn't had a good day in twenty years.

"How'd it go?" I ventured to ask.

He sucked in his breath and avoided eye contact. "As expected. An official petition to visit the archives has been filed."

"Do you think they'll grant you access?"

"Not to me, no."

He strode to the kitchen. I scooted down the couch to get a better view.

I raised my voice. "I'm sorry, I'm confused. Why did you file it then? You wanted to make the Council suspicious just to be denied?"

"The petition wasn't filed on my behalf," he said, coming

back from the kitchen with a bottle of sparkling water.

"I see. Kirsi?"

"Not her. Someone else. A person not easily connected to me."

"Okay, that was clever," I granted. "So, when they get it approved, we head to Alaska?"

He took off his jacket. He wore a black button-down shirt and black pants, like the first day we met. "No," he said as he sat down next to me. "If the petition is approved, we won't go. The person who filed it will."

Did I hear him right? "What? What's the whole point then?"

He cleared his throat. "I can see you need this explained. If the petition is approved, you can rest assured there are no prisoners in the dungeons of the vault and, therefore, no reason to go there at all."

"So, we'll go if the petition is denied?"

He nodded. "Eureka!"

"Okay, that kind of makes a little sense," I conceded, "but why must all you Shadows be such condescending pricks about everything?"

He closed his eyes. "You're comparing me to him. Great."

"The flaw in this brilliant plan is the waiting," I said. "We don't have to wait for your Immortal crony to call. We could just get on a plane to Alaska and once there, feel things out."

"I have a much better plan," Winter assured me.

"Oh? And what would that be?"

"We wait."

"See, you're a prick."

"Yeah," he said, facetiously. "I see that now."

I rubbed my temples to soothe my energy. "Listen, there are things happening, things you don't know, Jonas. I talked with a friend from the Deep Down today. A troglodyte convoy brought news of a dark alliance."

He took a moment to consider my words. "What friend?"

"A true friend. A childhood friend," I assured him. "She's a warrior."

Winter nodded three times but did not speak.

"Tam said elite troglodyte forces and their notorious General have broken away to partner up with wielders of dark magic."

"Interesting," he said, completely disinterested.

I felt like banging my head. "We're not going to do anything?"

"We'll monitor the situation and we'll train, something I should have been doing with you for years."

I rolled my eyes. "You Immortals move too slow. You've been ruined by an overabundance of time. You want to train when it's time to act."

"No, it's time to train," he said. "It's always time to train for the witch who wants to stand up against forces far greater than she can fathom."

I sighed. Maybe I needed the distraction. "What did you have in mind?"

He rubbed his chin. "What indeed? Anything and every-thing. You're so behind and so unskilled it's not even funny."

"Always with the compliments."

"We could work on your shields," he said. "You waste too much energy trying to control your flow. Unless you are hyper efficient, your shields will begin to break down during long battles. Unfortunately, shield efficiency training is very time consuming."

I shrugged. "What's the point? I will always heal."

He looked at me, mildly irritated.

"Oh, c'mon, Jonas, I've seen you forego summoning shields and take bullets in the gut and I think I know why. Healing is faster and requires less of our energy reserves."

"You think you have it all figured out? Trust me, the day will come when a fortified shield will be your only defense against Eternals. Without a shield, they'd drink up all your blood with a straw."

What a lovely thought.

"Then, and since you brought it up, there is the question of your healing time," he went on. "To condition your body to automate and accelerate the mending process, you need to be more efficient. Go back to step one."

"You and your shield training," I said. "Do you have a sponsor or something?"

He was not amused. "The proper shield leads to the prop-er power which leads to optimum healing."

"Okay, we'll do shield training, but can we learn healing first?"

He furrowed his brow. "Fine, but you're not going to like it."

One glance at him and I put two and two together. "Oh, no, no way, I'm not going to hurt myself over and over to train. Certainly not now."

He regarded me with patient, sympathetic eyes like you would a toddler.

"Inflicting lethal damage yields the best results. I find it's easier to have someone assist with that."

I waved my hand impatiently. "Next one, please."

He looked self-satisfied. "You want to delay lesson one and lesson two, searching for what? Something easy? Something fun? You want to learn fighting skills, but those won't matter if you blow all your energy on subpar shields and therefore are struggling to heal."

Winter waited for me to respond. I thought he wanted me to go back to lesson one, but instead I did not respond at all. He huffed and then reached under the couch to pull out two swords.

He threw a sword up in the air and I caught it midflight.

"Connect to your blade," he said. "First fighting skill... how to channel emotion to boost your energy during a fight."

I held the sword high with two hands. Magic shot through my tingling fingers into the hilt. The blade began to shimmer with a red glow. Pins and needles pulsated through my entire body as a connective path was forged between me and the magic-infused sword.

"Good," Winter said. "You haven't forgotten. Now, you see the way the blade glows red? Different colors mean different things. Red is the color of readiness. It means your blade has connected to your nervous system and your magic is ready to strike."

I swung the sword with simple flicks of the wrists, feeling the untamed force of the glowing blade.

"You can use the tension of your emotions to feed the magic in your sword," Winter said. "Your blade will reflect which emotion in color."

He flipped about on his feet and landed a sharp blow to my right knee with his sword. Blood spilled out of the injured joint as ligaments and cartilage ruptured.

I crumpled to the floor, shrieking in pain. Fury and something that felt like a murderous rage flared up in my chest.

"You didn't have to fucking do that," I hissed through the pain.

Winter clanged his sword against the tip of my blade. "Look at that."

A vibrant purple sheen coated the blade, sparking. I flicked my wrist and jammed the sword inside Winter's thigh.

He collapsed next to me, somehow grinning while grunting.

"Purple is for anger," he said. He pointed at my knee that

was already in mending mode. "Faster regeneration, faster reflex time. Anger will give your magic a little extra juice, but it will also drain reserves faster, leaving you with nothing. You can't rely on that boost."

I was still too furious to respond.

He jumped to his feet. Hot red fire sparkled to life in his left palm. He grabbed my hand and pulled me close. The heat from the flames nearly licked the side of my face. I recoiled with a grunt.

My blade kicked against my palm, shimmering with a green glow.

"Green is for fear," he said.

The fact I had a natural aversion to pure fire conjured through chemical reactions hadn't escaped him. My fire fear wasn't very dignifying for a mist rider or a lunar witch for that matter, both of which could manipulate earth and elemental energy to create sparks and fireballs and electricity waves. It was none of those things—it was actual flames that lingered and could slowly burn your flesh down to bone that tapped into primal fear.

The flame in Winter's hand extinguished.

"Fear will serve you as well as anger," he said, "and the effects will last longer. Love, sadness, and the instinct to protect will also persist. Love is white, sadness blue. Yellow is for the instinct to protect and is perhaps the most persevering. At times the emotion won't come from you, but you will feel an abundance around you. When you sense the emotions of others, you can pluck them out of the air."

I rubbed my completely healed knee. "The way you pluck elemental magic? Is that a Shadow thing? Transforming energy found in nature into electric, kinetic and magnetic fields?"

"In part, yes."

"How did you learn that?"

He rubbed the handle of his sword. "It is forbidden for Shadows to speak about any part of their becoming."

Even Shadows have cheat codes, ones they'll never share.

"We're taking Chaos at his word about the vault, aren't we?" I said.

He wiped down his blade with an oiled cloth. "We are."

"Why?"

He finished with the cloth and tossed it aside. "Control your sword," he said, ignoring my question.

My sword assumed a faint purple glow. *Huh, that makes sense.* The good magistrate was a reliable source for anger.

"Nice try," I said, "but I want an answer. Why does Chaos know where Emmet is? How can an outlaw become privy to information when we failed? You're the one with access to the Immortal network, not him."

"Chaos has a personal network that is more reliable than ours."

That was a lot to take in. "How's that possible?"

He hesitated. Shadows never hesitated. I gathered he was battling against a strong instinct not to tell me.

He locked his eyes on mine. "One of the first Immortals to become Eternal was Horror," he said. "Horror went through the stages of Immortal, Magistrate, Shadow and Eternal within the span of a single millennium instead of the thousands of years it usually requires.

"Only 800 years into his tenure as Eternal, he became unpredictable and obsessed with power. He imagined conspiracies everywhere. He pushed his magic too far, sharpening it, expanding it, refining it to catastrophic levels."

He stopped to reconsider his decision to tell me.

"What, Winter? What did Horror do?"

He shut his eyes and shook his head before continuing. "He played with the principles of time, attempting to alter its flow. He disrupted the balance of power among the Eternals by gathering an army of supernatural creatures and giving them dark magic. It took almost two thousand years to realize he was behind all of it. The First Council of Eternal Beings under the Preceptor of Gods finally stripped him of his privileges and confined him to his chambers where he could not access the power and magic of the natural world. They spared him from the exile vortex because of his status as an original Eternal."

"And he just stays in his room?" I said, not buying it.

"It's not a room in a traditional sense and the Eternals have to expend an enormous amount of their power just to keep him contained."

"Sounds like ancient history. What's this have to do with now?"

"For centuries, Chaos was Horror's pupil and protégé. He learned to channel much of Horror's power. At the time, Chaos was feared even among Eternals. Horror had plans to groom him to become his right hand and chief Warlord of his fast-growing army. But then Chaos somehow enraged Horror. No one knew what happened, but Chaos had to flee the Eternal realm to avoid Horror's wrath, always knowing Horror would one day find him.

"But then Chaos's luck changed. Horror was imprisoned. Chaos had survived a sure death sentence and was then able to fill the void Horror left behind and regain a fraction of the powers he had lost when he fled. The degrading scenario Chaos endured has left him frenetic and uncontrollable. Every joke he makes is a bitter joke. Part of Horror's magic, and what made him so lethal, was that his supernatural vision could see through time and space."

"The third-eye vision?"

"Exactly," Winter said. "*Revelations through veils of mist.* That's what Horror had called them. Chaos had just started to learn that skill when he had to flee for his life."

"Wait, so Chaos can see through time?"

"To some degree," Winter said, clearly unsure. "But he must be careful not to use too much of Horror's unique abilities, or there is the risk that he may obliterate his own essence. They are unstable energies, even when Horror himself used them and, worst of all, Horror can sense when his tricks are being co-opted. You could say that the fear of Horror still haunts every move Chaos makes. It's the only reason he shows any restraint whatsoever."

"Well, aren't we lucky?"

"In what sense?" he said, seriously.

"Never mind, I get sarcastic when I'm terrified."

"It's not appropriate."

"I realize that now."

"Good," he said. "To circle back to your question, it is my guess Chaos used that power to locate your wolf."

"The third-eye time vision thing?"

"Are you paying attention? *Yes.* And you are the only reason he would take such an immense risk."

Finally, a man who'd risk everything for me. Sheesh.

"Aren't I just the belle of the ball?"

"Sarcasm again?" he said, losing patience. "Humor is a form of weakness, an infantile psychological ruse used to escape existence."

"Sounds like good magic to me," I quipped, knowing I shouldn't have.

"You try my patience," he said. "Listen to me, daft girl, Horror's element is fire. He has controlled it since the beginning of Immortal time."

Fire again. I literally shivered. "And Chaos?"

He sighed. "Don't know. What I do know is that, for now, he wants nothing more than to be on your good side. Make no mistake, Luna. He will not hesitate to turn against you when he alters his objectives."

Of that I had no doubt. "Is Chaos more powerful than you?"

Winter slid his sword into its sheath.

"I mean you're both Immortals and Shadows," I went on, "but he's also Horror's one-time protégé apparently."

He fixed me in the coldest stare I'd ever felt. "What are you asking?"

My heart pounded in my chest. Adrenaline surged. "Would you really be able to protect me if Chaos comes for my head?"

His eyes dropped and his shoulders relaxed. "He would never do that when I was there. I think you know that. That is why you must train, Luna. It is the only way I can protect you when that final battle comes."

Everything inside me felt raw.

Winter's phone buzzed. He walked out to the balcony to answer.

The magic in my blood yearned to call on the moon and the west winds to rush in and create a cyclone of energy—for what end I did not know.

A cold breeze drifted over my shoulders and neck as the glass door to the balcony slid open and Winter stepped back inside.

"It is done," he said. "Petition denied."

I shook off the cold. "Good. Now let's go to Alaska."

"It's not going to be that easy," he said. He sat next to me and took my hand. "We can't get to the vault via any basic transportation methods. They can locate us at any airport now. They control everything. And we have to get there faster than basic technology can travel."

"What's happening, what are you trying to say?"

"Luna, we need to get there before the Seventh Council sets up additional safeguards caused by the petition. We must use the ley lines. We must travel via kinetic forces."

"What now? That's not even a thing," I said, panic setting in. "The Lunar Order has specifically forbidden it. Witches have died that way, I mean right on the spot, like zap and you're toast. Dead. No way. Think of something else."

Ley lines carried enormous amounts of raw, unrefined energy that shredded anyone who knew how to step on them. A little bit of knowledge is a bad thing.

"May I remind you that you can't die?" Winter said. "You have nothing to worry about. I'm nearly invincible near ley line intersections. Shadows have absolute control of ley energy and can manipulate it in a myriad of ways."

"Now you see, all I heard there was when you said *nearly invincible*, that's not as reassuring as you think."

He sensed my hesitation. "Luna, you don't have to go. I'm willing to save the wolf on my own."

Yeah, that wasn't happening and he knew it. Ley lines weren't the only thing he could manipulate.

"Nah," I said, defiantly. "Whatever a Shadow can do, a mist rider can surely do better."

Winter grinned. "Now that was funny."

Chapter 18

THE CIVIC SNAKED ITS way through the steep, mountainous terrain. That badass car had unmatched fortitude or maybe Winter had put a spell on it. Every time I thought it would give out, it just kept going. I wondered if there was a realm of magical old Civics I had never heard about. Probably.

The ley line intersection ran through the Anza-Borrego desert park area eighty miles to the northeast. By the time we got there, it was after midnight.

The desert night sky, free of clouds and artificial light, was dotted with endless stars. Some asterisms, like the Big Dipper and Orion's Belt, I knew very well and had used their gravitational forces on occasion. Others I was seeing for the first time.

Now on foot, Winter led me down Sandstone Canyon, a slot canyon so narrow it could barely fit two people. Naked, rocky cliffs towered above us.

Winter cast a beam of light ahead of us. I followed the light, trying to avoid paranoid thoughts about being ambushed in such a tight space.

The canyon widened up as it bent around to the right. My ears buzzed like they were being swarmed by bees. Pressure mounted inside my throat and nose. I sneezed. I felt a hot liquid dripping onto my upper lip.

"You've got a nosebleed," Winter said, without so much as a glance. "It's the energy overload entering your bloodstream."

Each step increased the pressure. A piercing headache split my skull. My hands and feet tingled, shooting nerve pain into my limbs.

"Dominate the energy now," Winter advised me, "before we reach the ley line. It will be too hard to gain control then."

"I can't," I said, struggling to keep my teeth from chattering.

"You can, Luna. You took control of the Moon in its metamorphic phase as energy spilled down in torrents. You can handle the damn ley lines."

I closed my eyes and surrendered to the invading current of energy. I let it spill into my core of magic and felt how it bumped against my own elemental energy. The two forces began to blend. I drew in a deep breath and directed my magic to attack, anchoring the ley line energy with my strongest witchcraft.

The collision resonated in every fiber of my body. It knocked me back.

The nosebleed stopped. The buzzing faded. The pressure abated.

"I told you," Winter said, taking my hand.

The ground rumbled under our feet. The underlying current sparked and hummed—shimmering energy floated two feet above ground in a whirlpool of blue and green light. Intermittently, a visible vibration wobbled across the sides of the canyon. I squeezed Winter's hand, overwhelmed.

The ley line intersection lay a few feet ahead. I'd never been that close before. The excessive energy saturation burned like a knife in my gut even with my magic keeping it contained.

"What would this current do to a basic?" I asked, barely audible.

"Nothing," Winter said. "Measly creatures can't register such high energy levels. The same way bats can hear ultrasonic frequencies, but basics can't."

"Cool. Guess that makes me batgirl."

I unbuttoned my jacket and gripped the hilt of my sword. Thin, ash-colored steam poured out of the blade.

"It's the magic saturation," Winter said.

I stared at the flickering wave of magic ahead when Winter suddenly put his arms around me from behind, pulling me close. He gently helped me slide my sword back into its sheath, then interlaced his fingers with mine.

A sizzling energy vibrated in my stomach.

"We have to take the ley line to the north," he said. "There's only one way to climb on it. We must jump together, at precisely the same time, as if we were of one body. Otherwise, we might end up in different lanes and lose sight of each other. I fear you won't get to the Brooks Range on your own, so it is best to make sure we stay connected."

His warm breath tickled my ear, his strong hands gently enveloping mine. I leaned back, melding into his body, my back against his muscled chest. He pulled me even tighter until there was no molecule of air between us.

My heart skipped beats, lunging in my chest. I didn't know if it was the magic overload or the anxiety of the looming ley ride or the simple comfort of his warm body against mine.

"Ready?" he said. "We go on a count of three."

I nodded, my nerves fraying.

One... Two... Three!

We jumped. It was like crashing into a wall of steel. Everything hurt at once and I lost balance. Winter held me steady as the dark landscape flashed by at incredible speed. My stomach pushed into my throat, my vision blurred, and I was convinced my legs were gone, but I stayed conscious.

Little by little I regained feeling in my limbs. Apparently, I still had all four of them. The magic swirled around as in an eye of a hurricane. Winter's light beam reflected off everything at once like a strobe light.

My hands were beyond clammy, they were wet. Cold sweat oozed down my neck onto my back. Time distorted. I drifted into a trancelike state.

Winter nudged me. I startled. I wasn't sure if what was happening was real or just a very bizarre dream.

"We're switching lanes," he yelled, but I heard it like a whisper.

"What do you mean?"

"This ley line stops in Alberta. We have to go farther."

My daze deepened. He snatched me up into his arms and cradled me as if I were a child, pressing my face to his chest, and he leapt.

Another collision against a hard wall of energy squeezed my insides, draining me of feeling. I glanced at Winter. He was in perfect control of his faculties, his eyes focused somewhere far ahead, unblinking. It would take centuries, if ever, to get to that level of discipline.

We were violently stopped, then launched. Nothing hurt anymore. We landed softly on a cool cloud.

Winter's light extinguished, leaving us in the dark.

"What's this?" I said.

"End of the road."

I felt the ground underneath my butt. We were not in the sky; we had landed on snow. Deep, crisp snow that turned to ice on my palms.

Winter's light flashed back into life. He was standing,

scanning the area with his beam. "For a first-time rider, you did fine," he said. "I've seen Immortals empty their stomachs all over themselves."

I rubbed my arms, trembling. "It's so cold."

He knelt by my side. "It's Alaska and it's even colder around the Sacred Vault, but this is unusually low, colder than I've ever felt."

"I'm freaking freezing," I said through chattering teeth.

He took a wool blanket out of his backpack and wrapped me with it, then scraped ice off my hands before sliding a pair of gloves on them.

"I can withstand temperatures well below zero, but this is too cold even for me," he said, taking my boots off to rub my feet. "It could be me. The magic is heavy here and I'm carrying all that ley line energy. The combination of the two forces might be reacting to my etheric essence."

I thought about what he had just said. "My god, it's not just a name, is it? You *are* Winter."

He grinned while replacing my boots. "I am not a season of the year. I don't know Santa Claus, nor is Mother Nature my actual mother, but when it comes to icy climates, I'm your man."

I couldn't feel my toes or my fingers. "I do better in San Diego."

Winter hugged me to his chest and murmured something I didn't understand. Then he blew out a misty vapor that wrapped me up, warming me all the way to my bones like someone had lit a bonfire in my heart.

"Cool spell," I said. I laughed like an idiot. "Get it? See what I did?"

He nodded, not really amused, but less dismissive than usual.

"More of a warm spell," he said, distracted. "Going to the vault tonight is out of the question. The spell breaks fast if you don't stay in place. You'll freeze to death out there, again and again. We'll have to find shelter nearby, wait out the night when the ley energy dissipates."

"Wait, we'll approach the vault in broad daylight?"

"We are in Arctic Alaska. The morning will bring more darkness, then a little twilight by mid-morning. It makes no difference. It's not eyes who guard the vault's perimeter. It's a labyrinth of wards and shielding magic. Whether night or day, winter or summer, they would feel us coming."

"I'm not even going to ask, because you better have a plan to get in and another to get out with one of their prisoners, or I'll kill you."

My threats amused him far more than my jokes. "Let's hope my reinforced shield holds out," he said. "We know we can't rely on yours."

Yeah, because you mention it every five minutes!

I began feeling cold again. The vapor spell was weakening. He repeated the spell ritual and pulled me to my feet.

The fresh snow was knee deep. I struggled to walk up-hill in the darkness of the polar night. Even the sky looked bleak—the stars and the moon had been chased away by large, fat clouds.

Winter stopped in front of a drift of snow twelve feet high. He lowered his light to shine on an oval stone that had steam coming off it. I squatted to examine the runes engraved on it.

He placed his palm on the stone. His flesh sizzled and burned on the hot rock. A hissing breeze swirled around us, blowing the front of the drift clean away to reveal the dark mouth of a cave.

We followed Winter's light into the dark tunnel. The warm vapor spell vanished before we were twenty feet into the cave. The cold quickly chilled my bones.

The cave was wider than I expected, and its walls were unnaturally dry and smooth. Further in, the clear ground was covered with rope carpets.

At the back of the cave, rectangular bricks formed a circle.

Winter walked over to the circle and held his hand above it. Blue flames sparkled inside the brick pit like monster tongues, brightening our new home.

Heat reached me in waves and felt as soothing as warm bath water.

I exhaled, relieved. A shelter and a hearth can be intoxicating.

I noticed there was no smoke emanating from the fire. It wasn't oxygen burning, it was magic happening. That made it feel even more like home.

"I thought ice was your thing," I said with a grateful grin.

He took off his jacket and gloves. "The magic in this area is so potent even a basic could start a fire."

"Not really?"

"No, not a basic, but you get the idea."

He sat against the wall and waved me over. I sat next to him, keeping my coat zipped. I still had some thawing out to do. I felt like a popsicle.

"Get some sleep," he said.

"What about you?"

He shook his head. "No need. I'd rather be awake."

"We need you to be at your best," I insisted.

He took my gloved hand in his. "I have to warn you, Luna. If Emmet is there, we'll have to fight and kill to even get near him. You can stay here. I can go to the Sacred Vault alone. This is your last chance. Once we approach that place, there is no time to run. If you do not kill them, they will try to kill you and when you do not die, the whole bloody Immortal network will be informed."

I felt sick. "Is it necessary?"

"More than necessary," he said. "We can't leave any witnesses."

My stomach contracted. I swallowed down the urge to vomit.

He rubbed my back. "It's the only way."

"Tell me they're all evil at least," I said. "We're just going to kill everyone?"

"If they don't capture us first. Luna, stay here. I'll get the wolf."

Was Emmet's life more important than all those guards, or any single guard for that matter? Was mine? Was Winter's?

"They are on the wrong side of history," he said.

"They are just following orders."

"Some of those orders include abduction and torture."

I knew that if I survived it all, I would never be the same, but I would not abandon a friend to be carved up in a house of horrors.

"I'm going," I said. "I came here to get Emmet."

"That's good, because I could use the help."

I punched his chest. "You idiot."

The big goon smiled. I rested my head on his shoulder. "I'm not sure I ever thanked you for helping. Without you, I wouldn't have had a chance and Emmet would be lost."

"Thank me when the wolf is free."

I felt sleepy and oddly content. "Tell me about my real family."

He pursed his lips and stared at the fire. I saw a twitch in his jaw and his gaze drop to the ground. "You're better off not knowing."

Of course, he said that. "Maybe that's for me to decide."

His eyes hardened. "Maybe, but you'll never hear it from me. It would put you in danger and not just you, those who love you. Let it be, Luna."

"You're not the only one who knows, are you?"

He turned and put his warm hand on my cold cheek. When he lifted his eyes to mine, they were fathomless. It was like being seen from thousands of years at once. "I learned long ago, we are not our families. We build ourselves one day at a time, one decision at a time. I watched you grow up. You already have a family and you have defined yourself."

"That's cute," I said, getting sleepy. "Sounds like a fortune cookie."

I rested my head on his shoulder again. I liked it.

"I take that as a compliment," he said. "In my earliest centuries, I spent many springs of the Zhou dynasty chatting with Sun Tzu."

"Dynasties are from a long time ago," I said, falling asleep.

Chapter 19

WHEN MY EYES OPENED, something soft was tucked under my head. Winter's parka jacket. I looked around the cave. He wasn't there. He must have gone outside, plotting our next move.

I tried to sit up as gently as possible. The blue fire was still burning but not as bright. I had no idea what time it was. I pulled my backpack onto my lap and took the flip phone out.

It was ten fifteen in the morning. There was no service, but the number 8 flashed on the screen—eight messages that must have arrived sometime last night before we got on the ley line express. I probably was too anxious to hear the faint buzzing of the old phone.

The first message was a coupon from Panera Bread. Faion and I ordered food from the restaurant on New Year's Day.

The remaining seven were all from Lily.

Where r u? Police called here 2x

U gave them Lucia's number

Want u to call ASAP

witness came 4ward

Cop was cute!

Witness had Jonas at your place

On day of vandals!!!

Uncle Viking circled your home,

then entered!!

Confirming footage from traffic light cam!

CYA, Sophie!! HMB ASAP

I stared at my phone. It made no sense. Cameras weren't supposed to work around Winter, and he could easily block the function of all electronic devices. He would never be so careless. He left nothing to chance. No way.

And yet, there was a witness and footage.

Had he deceived me again? Would I ever stop being his pawn?

What did make sense, and it shouldn't really surprise me, was that he would stop at nothing to pull me back inside his orbit. He had invested way too much time in grooming a mist rider to do his bidding. Maybe he thought I was his ticket to finally beating Chaos at his own game. I didn't know. All I knew was that his enthusiasm at the prospect of having me under his thumb again could have made him sloppy.

I had to tread lightly. Maybe some part of me wanted him to be guilty. Maybe I needed to express some lingering hostility and his guilt allowed that.

Right on cue, he walked in, lugging a bucket of snow. "Good, you're awake," he said with a smile. "How long have you been up?"

I glanced at the phone. "Long enough to see through your deception."

He set the bucket down and rubbed his neck. "What now?"

"You tell me. Have you been feeding me lies again?"

"What kind of lies?"

"Ah, you have different kinds," I snapped. "Well, let's see. The San Diego Police can place you outside my apartment right before it was trashed."

His eyes narrowed. "No, they can't," he said, emphatically.

"Did you have a nightmare?"

"Don't even start. Look for yourself."

I handed him the phone so he could see the texts.

He didn't miss a beat. "It's fake. What reason would I have?"

"I don't know, here we are, you and I alone in a cave at the end of the world like some superhero crime fighting duo. Your wish realized. And the best part is, when this was all over, I'd be forever in your debt."

He flared his nostrils. "Except I didn't kidnap the wolf, nor did I trash your place. And I know you know that."

"I don't know that. The police have the evidence."

He leaned forward, irritation sparking his irises. "Believe what you want. I'll give you a few minutes to collect yourself. When I return, we'll go over the plan one last time and leave for the vault."

He took off. Every nerve in me tightened.

"Don't you dare walk out on me."

He slowed before the mouth of the cave for a moment, then walked out without looking back.

My hand twitched. Something fierce stirred in my blood. The energy blast left my hand almost of its own accord. Maybe it was the dense web of magic of that damned vault or the powerful ley line residual energy or my mist rider core. I didn't know and I didn't care. There was no force on Earth able to halt the mega upsurge of power that escaped my body.

The energy field hit Winter just as he had stepped out into the mid-morning Alaskan twilight. It enveloped him like a simmering dome made of transparent, crisscrossing electromagnetic forces, trapping him and dragging him back inside the cave.

He spun inside the halo of finely threaded energy I had crafted. He glared at me with a predatory certainty that promised great violence.

He became curious, reaching out to touch the halo. His hands smoked and blistered on the spot. He'd burn himself into a crispy skeleton if he tried to escape my magic.

He bent over, burying his face in both hands. When he stood tall again, his aggression had vanished. He stepped back carefully to give himself room, then stretched his healed hands out in front of him. His body vibrated wildly from head to toe as coils of energy rolled about the dome, splitting it open.

My energy collapsed with a roaring thud. Searing pain cut through my skull, so sharp it momentarily blinded me.

Too late did I realize Winter had worked up a shield already. He looked smug and pleased with himself, and maybe a little tired, too.

Fucking A-hole.

I pulled myself together. "I can break it," I declared, defying him.

He flashed his white teeth. "Bring it on, little witch."

For a second, I hesitated. A voice inside my head told

me I was no match for Winter. Not yet. Then the magic buildup crested again, and I let all my might rise within me. My electric field encircled Winter's shield, creating a sizzling circuit. Elemental energy pulsated out of my cells, gnawing at the threads of his translucent shield.

He watched me from within the shield, his eyes shining.

I kept my assault as steady as possible, gradually increasing intensity.

Nothing. I accomplished nothing. Not a single superficial crack. I had expended an enormous amount of my resources without gaining an inch.

I remembered my lesson. His shields were impermeable. I knew it. He knew it. Assaulting them head on was a terrible idea. I was driven by pure anger and anger was a temporary boost that left you with nothing.

I searched within my core for a connection to the closest ley line. I found an open path and locked onto it. I drew the ley line energy slowly towards the cave like a cat sneaking up on its tiptoes.

The ground under Winter's feet quaked. He took a step backwards as the floor cracked, chunks of it sinking. The electromagnetic force of the ley line shot upwards and exploded inside his shield.

He was swept up into the air, smashed his head against the cave's roof, then dropped to the ground with a thud.

When he climbed to his feet, he laughed.

Huh?

My energy deflated like a balloon. The connection to the ley line was cut. The instant I tried to restart the connection, I slammed against a barrier of forbidding magic. Winter had now taken full control of the ley line.

Uh oh.

His eyes flashed purple. *The color of anger.*

The back of my neck bristled. The look on his face was murderous. He charged at me. I panicked, putting up a flimsy shield that he punched back instantly. He grabbed my wrist and spun me to the ground. Before I knew it, he was on top of me, straddling me.

He took my face in his hands. "I did not kidnap the wolf shifter. I'm here because you asked me to help."

I kneed his groin, causing strain in his features. He pinned my hands above my head. "For the last time, I am not the enemy."

He turned his head slightly to the left. The skin on his neck was warm and smelled like fresh air and peppermint. Something took over and I sank my teeth in, biting into him like a vampire. He grunted and let go of my hands. I pushed him off me, but it was like pushing a dead bear.

"What are you kinky kids up to?"

Winter rolled to the side. I sat up. Chaos was leaning against the cave entrance, hands in his pockets, the hilt of his sword peeking over his shoulder.

We looked at him with daggers.

"A lovers' spat perhaps?" he went on.

"You're in on it, too, aren't you?" I said.

He crunched his face. "*In on it*? The English language is phonetically unrefined."

Chaos stepped around mounds of tundra and exploded rocks to glance down at the gaping hole in the Earth.

"Tsk, tsk, tsk," he said. "Someone had a dangerous bit of fun."

Winter pounced on Chaos from behind, running him into the wall. Chaos spun around, but Winter kept his hand around his throat. With his free hand, Winter pointed two fingers directly into Chaos's eyes.

"Oh, good gracious, no, he wants to draw my essence out," Chaos said, amused though choking. "Help, Luna, I'm so scared."

Winter squeezed Chaos's throat harder. His aura began to vibrate and deepened to a blinding purple.

Chaos coughed. "Tell me, little dove, what am I supposed to be *in on*?"

"Kidnapping Emmet, obviously, so you two old perverts can pull me back into your sadomasochistic rivalry. You probably made a bet who could win my favor because you're bored after living so long."

Chaos's brows crept up. "You think Mr. Warmth here had something to do with the Emmet Groshek kidnapping? As tempting as it would be to egg you on, no, it's not him. This one does not value complexity and his obsession with you makes him painfully predictable."

"Is this your confession?" I asked.

Steam sprang forth and took Chaos. When he reappeared, he was standing by the fire pit, flashing his pearly whites.

"You wonder how I did that," he said. "Your noble magistrate let me do it, sugar muffin. He likes that I've come to his defense."

Winter stood by the entrance. Chaos lingered in the back. I felt more than a little contained. Alone in an arctic cave with two deranged shadows may not be the ideal space on Earth for a mist rider to occupy.

"Whatever you think you know, you don't," Chaos said in a sing-song voice as if singing a lullaby. "The culprit will always cover her tracks."

"*Her* tracks?" I said, intrigued. "You think a woman is the kidnapper? Where did you come by your information?"

He raised his hands in surrender. "I'm just being politically correct, honey bunch. You newborn souls nowadays get your knickers in a bundle over gender pronouns and the lot."

What bullshit.

"Nice try, but you two putting your sick heads together makes more sense. That would explain why you jump to each other's defense so quickly even though you supposedly disagree on everything else."

Chaos chuckled. "A disagreement? That's what you've come up with? That the esteemed magistrate and I disagree? We've had a frightful tiff? Did you hear that, Winter, perhaps we've shown bad form at a dinner party?"

I turned to Winter. "You're quiet. Are you enjoying this?"

"He is," Chaos said. "Saw him smirking at the bit about the dinner party."

Now I glared at Winter, who still wasn't speaking.

"Trying to cool down," he said.

"I didn't think cold-hearted bastards needed to cool down," I said. "Forget this Immortal's rambling. I need you to explain yourself."

Winter exhaled hard through his nostrils. "I monitored your apartment when you were gone. That happened. I anticipated the location might become a target and that it should be monitored."

Chaos sneered. "Do you ever listen to yourself talk, mate? I love to hear you talk, no, really. I've missed you. It's been, what? Five centuries?"

Winter ignored him. "I was not there during the attack, but I now see that the attack was a catalyst not only for the kidnapping but to create suspicions between us. The same plan brought us here."

Chaos nodded. "Major, major clusterfuck."

"Here, you can feel my truth," Winter said.

He clutched my hand and slid it under his shirt, my palm against his breastbone. I felt his strong heartbeat and something wilder, like an explosion of ice particles deep inside his chest. An electric current shocked my hand and now I saw something, a kind of vision. Winter's mind opened to me like a lotus flower, crystalized images sliding before my eyes like a kaleidoscope. Every pulse of his conscience screamed innocence.

"Is this a *Me Too* moment?" Chaos quipped under his breath.

Winter let go of my hand. It fell to my side, lifeless. I knew he was telling the truth. For an instant, he let a connective path link us and I absorbed his most intimate feelings. The experience was unnerving and felt unreal, but in my gut, I knew absolutely it was true.

We faced each other. I wanted to apologize but not with Chaos there.

"Don't stop on my account," Chaos said. "I was going to snap a photo."

I gave him the stink eye. "Why are you even here? I distinctly remember you refusing to help."

"Well, I'm here as a neutral observer, butter biscuit, and to be honest, there was exactly shit on the Telly. *Hoarders* is my show. I might have been the world's first hoarder, you know. Had to give it up. No room to walk."

He laughed like a madman before he vanished, this time for good.

What a total jackweasel!

"Immortals watch TV?" I asked Winter.

The question surprised him. "Of course, we do. It's the Golden Age."

Chapter 20

We climbed up a snow-covered bluff all the way to the top. The Noatak River stretched down the other side, its surface a glossy green in the dim twilight.

It wasn't anywhere near as cold as when the ley line dumped us in the middle of nowhere, but still far colder than anything I had ever experienced, and that included Whitehorse, Yukon.

I wore three thermal shirts, wool leggings, two sweaters, ski pants, two pairs of gloves, three pairs of socks and a jacket so puffy I must have looked like a fat astronaut.

Walking in that gear wasn't easy. I wobbled awkwardly with each step (again, like a fat astronaut), but at least I didn't freeze to the bone.

We reached the river, then followed it for a while in silence.

Thin layers of ice floated down the winding river, glistening.

"You showed great command of the ley line in the cave," Winter said. "I wasn't in the mood at the time to comment."

"Thanks, I guess," I said. "I was having a mood myself."

"Well, I take pride in your progress."

"Like fatherly pride?" I said and immediately regretted it. Why the hell did I say that? It'd be better to keep my mouth shut from now on.

Winter frowned. "Not so much fatherly. I have no experience with that kind of emotional construct."

"In what way then?" I insisted.

It took him a while to answer. "In my way, call it a friend's way."

I chuckled. "Really? That's what we are? Friends?"

"Let's call it a mentor's pride then," he said.

I grabbed his hand. "Winter," I said. "Over there."

A pair of boots protruded from behind a snow-covered boulder.

Winter scanned the entire area before moving slowly toward the boulder. I followed, readying my energy. Winter tensed and crouched as he reached the rock and then... relaxed.

Three bodies lay behind the boulder, their limbs intertwined. They wore brass armor with intricate patterns—their sleeves and pant legs were green.

Winter turned them over on their backs one by one. The

skin on their hands was reptilian and their faces a pale olive green with large, protruding lower jaws and aquiline noses but no ear lobes.

Troglodytes.

The front of their necks had been cut open and their throats torn out. Long serrated gashes ran from their chests down to their lower abdomens.

They were completely emptied out. All vital organs had been removed.

"Ritual killings," Winter said, pensively.

An ugly memory resurfaced. "Just like at the *Palacio de Taxidermia.*"

A loud splash echoed from the river. We turned around. Rippling circles grew larger and larger on the water's surface.

Winter dropped his backpack and shed his clothes quickly. "I'll see what that was about."

"You'll freeze to death," I protested.

He stood in his boxer briefs, grinning. "I'm confident neither is possible."

"You don't know what's in there, Jonas."

"Whatever's in there," he said as he walked, "it can't be worse than me."

I grabbed his hand before he could run to the river.

"I'll be fine," he said. "It's nice to know you worry about me."

"I'm worried about myself," I corrected him. "I'd be lost out here without you. You know, if you were kidnapped, or if you got hypothermia. You already have goose pimples."

I tried to warm him by wrapping my arms around him, but it was impossible inside my hundred layers of clothing.

"You'd be lost without me?" he said as he aided my attempt to warm him by wrapping me up in his long arms and pulling me close. "How about a goodbye kiss?" He paused, big grin on his face. "In case I don't make it back."

I stared up into his eyes, and the world started spinning. Suddenly, his lips touched mine and I panicked, but then I kissed him back. It was me who escalated it from a gentle peck to my tongue searching for his tongue... finding his tongue... swirling playfully around his tongue.

Oh my god, what am I doing?

He had kissed me once before, but his fervor still knocked my socks off. The man tasted so good, like an explosion of nectar and honey and watermelon juice. Maybe it had something to do with his immortality, or maybe it was all him, Winter, Jonas Sandell, the shadow I couldn't escape.

I didn't know how such a soft kiss could feel so savage. We pretended our lives were in imminent danger, and maybe they were, but it was all a playful excuse. This was a one-time, no, a two-time thing, nothing more.

I'll keep telling myself that.

He pulled away first. I wobbled on my feet like a drunk duck. He caught me before I fell on my butt, then ran to the river and dove into the icy water.

I watched as his head disappeared under the water, his

taste still on my lips. Nothing compared to his kisses—absolutely nothing.

I folded his clothes, mechanically, the whole time watching the water like a hawk. Seconds went by, then minutes that felt like a little eternity.

Winter resurfaced, carrying a black trash bag. His carved pecs and ripped abdomen glistened like gold in the twilight. I threw a blanket around him.

He dropped the bag down and used the blanket to dry himself. He crouched to untie the bag. A pile of bloody innards spilled out, turning the pristine snow suddenly scarlet. I yelped and backed away.

"I'm going to throw up," I said.

He shook water drops off his hair and looked around, sniffing the air.

"Who did this?" I said. "Why?"

He started to get dressed. "Don't know. My concern is that these creatures were here at all."

"My concern is whoever did this to them."

"I don't like the way the river smells," he said. "We have to be quick."

I followed him along the river's edge, patiently waiting for him to talk.

"I don't know what we'll find at the vault," he said. "Be ready. You'll need to summon all available energy around you, be it from the sky or the earth or from your core. Stay close. Do not hold back. Do not show mercy. I assure you they have no mercy for you. Growing new organs is not a good time."

I preferred staying silent until that last bit. "Wait, you mean I could survive that kind of slaughter?"

"Yes, but you'd wish you had died. It can take days to regrow a liver when there's not a shred of one left. In the meantime, you'll live like you're in the final stages of cirrhosis."

I'm converted. No mercy.

We walked quietly for the better part of an hour until we came to a log cabin among tall, leafless trees. I felt the dense energy of Winter's shield for the first time. He must have reinforced it.

He studied me from head to toe. "You can't fight like that," he said. "We'll hide a few layers of that here."

I took off layer after layer. I stopped when I was down to leggings and a thermal shirt. I bundled the rest inside the jacket. Winter dug a hole on the side of the cabin and placed the bundle and our backpacks inside, covering them with snow.

We stood outside the cabin's door. Winter zapped the door handle with a single finger. The lock clicked and the door swung open. The interior was bare—nothing but a table with a chair and a trapdoor on the floor.

Winter lifted the trapdoor. We stepped carefully down the wooden steps into darkness. A portal shimmered to life at the bottom of the stairs. Without a word, Winter took my hand and we stepped through the portal.

We started to fall through a cold dark space, completely protected by Winter's energy shield. I clutched onto his hand to stay oriented.

A dim light met us as our feet landed softly in a coiling passageway walled in by red bricks. I thrust a beam of light ahead as we prepared to journey into the unknown. My heart sunk as around curve after curve the passageway never seemed to end.

Winter brought his index finger to his lips. I nodded and followed him. We came to another bend. As we rounded the bend, a pack of at least twenty troglodytes came running at us armed with swords and spears.

White energy glowed at my fingertips. I raised my hands and—

"Halt!" A resounding male voice filled the space.

The troglodytes came to a sudden stop, as if stunned by Tasers.

They stood at attention ten feet from us. Every last troglodyte focused their eyes on me, slit pupils gleaming yellow, unblinking. In a moment, they lowered their weapons and, as one, snorted hard out of their noses.

At the back of the group, I caught a glimpse of the tall troglodyte who had barked out the order. He was armored in red with a golden helmet. He peered into my eyes, lifted his hand, gestured, then the troglodytes spun about and marched off at double time, then started running.

I looked to Winter who just shook his head.

We pressed forward. A few minutes later a larger group of guards rounded a bend a hundred feet away. They marched in formation, wearing helmets with horns and long chain-mail coats. They were short and bulky, carrying axes and cleavers. They looked like a dwarf army without the beards. Their auras shone orange, drenched with magic.

What in the world are they?

Confusion swept their faces when they spotted us. They slowed to consider what threat we posed. One among the front row reached for something under his armor.

By instinct, I hurled an energy ball that struck his hand and knocked him back into the second row of guards.

They were unfazed and began marching again as one, raising their axes that were sparking with orange energy.

Their aggression magic bit at my skin like tiny sharp needles. Drops of blood rolled down my cheeks and hands.

These were battle powers I thought only existed in myths.

As the dwarf legion approached, I blasted them. My blasts crashed into a barrier before hitting them. The pack had put up an energy shield.

I backed away, desperate to locate the source of the shield. There he was, without an axe, at the left of the pack.

Think again if you're planning to beat me at my game!

Channeling every available resource, I assaulted their shield with heavy waves of energy, testing its limits.

The shield howled as magic blew through its essence,

draining its potency.

The wielder strained to keep his shield in place. My blasts expanded wider and wider and struck the shield from every possible angle.

Wait, am I in this alone?

No. Winter was in fact here, yet the bastard leaned back against the tunnel wall, a casual smile painted on his mug.

"Anytime you're ready to help..."

"No need," he said. "You got this."

Are you fucking serious right now?

The pack began to move as one, taking long strides. Magic jumped from their hands onto their weapons, studding them with long spikes.

Thirty feet away.

The shield around the pack hissed and cracked.

Winter did provide a little extra anger. I charged.

Twenty feet.

The dwarves began howling, breaking formation.

Ten feet.

By the time I reached them, the shield crack had widened. I leapt right through it. I hit the ground and skidded, until I crashed into thick legs.

I could hear my own bones crunching. As I got up in pain, an axe swung past my head. I ducked just in time, whipped around and sliced at chainmail with a whip of energy. The dwarf fell, a bloody gash across his chest.

The murderous dwarves came one and all. I blasted left

and right, but it was hopeless. There were too many. If I somehow survived, my last kill would be Winter, the smug prick. That became my main motivation. To survive just so I can slice him to pieces.

I was bludgeoned from behind, the impact knocking me forward. My destroyed shoulder had been burned clean through the shoulder blade.

Tears blurred my vision. My hand went numb.

I turned back to find a spiky axe looming above my head, ready to crush my skull. I felt magic dripping from the axe. I quickly cloaked it in my own magic a heartbeat before it split my skull.

When the two magic waves collided, they exploded.

The shockwave knocked everyone back. My head struck the floor. The walls closed in as my vision drowned in blood and tears. I struggled to keep breathing. My wounds were everywhere.

Winter's voice found me as if from within a dream. "Lethal force, witch."

Yeah, I knew it would come to that. He didn't help because he wanted me to do the killing.

Before I had decided, a colossal wave of power surged within. It was coming at me from everywhere at once, the earth's underbelly, the sky above, the bricks and the trees and the stars and my own blood.

The dwarves pounded on me, slicing my flesh. I realized I had been screaming the whole time. Now I put all my rage into my screams, piercing my own eardrums and killing everything, except Winter.

I felt a jolt of dark euphoria—ending all those life forces had made me lust for more energy, more power. I raised all the dwarf corpses high above me. Covered in blood, my own and theirs, I stared at my handiwork. For the first time, I felt like something else, something beyond Sophie, beyond Luna, beyond all I had known or imagined, beyond even good and evil.

I let go. The bodies smacked against the ground, piling up in front of me.

Is this what I am now? Death?

Winter wrapped an arm around my shoulders. I felt a new kind of cold, a cold his warmth could never chase away. I felt alone, I felt the absence of an eventual end. I felt unreachable. I felt... immortal.

I buried my face in Winter's neck and breathed in his fresh scent. He stroked my hair and held me tight. My wounds were mending. I would always heal while others died.

"Okay," I said, collecting myself. "We have to find Emmet."

Winter helped me to my feet. "None of these creatures had any business being here," he said. "These are strange times. They are not the usual guards."

"Why did the troglodytes run?"

Winter hesitated. "They knew they couldn't fight you."

The troglodytes had known me before I knew me. Perhaps

they were saving me for the dark lord of the soul swallowers himself.

Winter led me to a winding staircase. At the bottom, we found a large rotunda flooded with blinding light. Rows of doors lined the walls.

We walked to massive wooden double doors. A metal plaque read:

Eternal Archives and Registry of the Forbidden Vortex

"Emmet," I said, my heart booming.

Hold on, Emmet. We're here.

Chapter 21

THE DOOR WAS GUARDED by a massive number of spells and wards. That was bad enough, but according to Winter they were rigged, so that removing any one of them would trigger all the others.

A quagmire of epic proportions. Any attempt to mess with the ward system would lead to a detonation surely to obliterate everything in the archival rotunda and all the tunnels that led to it.

The records in the vault would vanish and the vault itself would collapse, killing any non-immortals inside—including Emmet.

"You better know what you're doing with these," I told Winter.

He nodded. "I do, you will break them."

Excuse me?

"You can't seriously think I'm the person for the job. You're thousands of years old. I'm not even twenty-three yet."

"You will be in four months, two weeks, three days and, let me see…" He took a wind-up watch out of his pocket. "Five hours and seventeen minutes."

I glared at him. "Dude, don't be a Stan."

"Stan?"

"*Stalker* slash *Fan*. That's you, a *Stan*."

He became curious. "It's an insult?"

"You can handle it," I said. "You can also handle this door. I have no skill or even a frame of reference on how to hack elaborate ward combinations, especially ones that didn't even originate in the Deep Down."

"It's within your capabilities," he said.

"You're nuts. My training with wards ended when I was a child, when I chose to live in the up above. That was eight years ago. We were learning how to break cookie jar wards back then. Not this."

"You can't train for everything," he said. "This is between you and your magic. Nothing else."

"Well, I appreciate that vote of confidence, but choosing me when we have you is utter bullshit."

"There's a lot of utter bullshit in all the realms," he said, then sat down cross-legged. He wasn't going to move a muscle until I gave it a shot.

I opened my palms. "You're really not doing this?"

He didn't answer, just assessed the state of his fingernails.

"What a freaking dick," I said to myself, but he could still hear.

I calmed my breathing and closed my eyes. The only thing I knew for sure was that you needed to sense the wards to break them. Eventually, some patterns emerged but they meant little to me. I couldn't locate the mechanism behind the origin of the protective spells. That was step one. Dealing with interlinked wards was an unknown step I never learned anything about.

"Nope," Winter said. "You're going about it the wrong way."

I opened my eyes. "Makes sense, because I don't know what the hell I'm doing."

"Don't search for the wards, show them what *you* are."

"And how do I do that exactly?"

He sighed. "Don't hide from this, Luna. You were born for it."

Not knowing what the hell he was on about, I decided to show the wards the only two things I knew about myself. My bloodline and my heritage.

I glanced about the rotunda. Two crossed swords hung in a glass case on the wall. Their hilts were studded with precious stones, which formed the legendary double-headed eagle that had served as an emblem and a heraldic symbol for Immortals for centuries.

With a snap of my fingers, I imploded the glass and

grabbed a sword.

I held out my hand to the door and slashed the blade across my wrist. Blood spurted from my veins like a fountain, drenching the wards and the door they guarded.

For a moment, nothing. Then the wards flickered and hissed like oil in a hot skillet.

Beams of color exploded in rainbows all over the room—reds, yellows, browns, blues, greens and oranges, in every shade ever imagined.

A wispy ground mist climbed up the door, wrapping the wards gently. The wards expanded and contracted, again and again, every time losing some of their density.

The mist whistled and swelled, licking up every last morsel of color and energy contained in the wards.

I glanced at Winter, stunned and exhilarated at the same time. I had heard some legends about the mist magic of the morning people, a.k.a. the mist riders, which could penetrate and conquer every type of supernatural force, and now I had been able to conjure it.

So damn cool.

I tried the handle on the door. It was locked. *With an actual lock.*

"Do you have a spell for that?" I asked Winter.

He chuckled, then took a running start to ram his shoulder into the door and break the lock.

That works, too.

It was pitch dark inside. A smell of old paper and brandy

hit my nostrils as we took a few steps into the vault.

"Ouch," I yelped. Something sharp nipped at my right side.

I rubbed my stinging flesh and heard the hurried shuffling of feet.

Winter's hand found mine.

"What happened?"

"Felt like something pinched me."

"Pinched you?"

Winter flipped a switch. Orange light flooded the space around us.

"Some small creature—" I started to say but then shut my mouth.

A vast library stood before us. Floor after floor of ancient bookshelves spiraled upward as far as my eyes could see.

Marble floors, silver and gold detailing, wrought-iron sculptures and spectacular painted walls that depicted natural settings took my breath away.

Narrow passageways and staircases ran along the length and height of the library, connecting everything in an elaborate pattern.

Every book, every story, every dissertation ever written must have found its place in that colossal underground construction.

"I'll disarm the fields protecting the shelves," Winter said and walked off.

I moved about the floor, light on my feet, mindful not to

disturb anything, remembering the famous fire in Alexandria that had destroyed so many texts from the ancient world. All those texts might still be here in the many ancient libraries of the Sacred Vault.

Something sparked and flickered on a nearby shelf like the dying wick of a candle. Pushing aside Volume I of *Andalusian Dark Arts in the Middle Ages*, I found an enchanted kaleidoscope flashing. I touched it—the shelf whirled about itself so fast that it blended with the wall behind it. When the spinning stopped, a door stood ajar where the bookshelf had been.

After a moment of hesitation, I walked through the door, taking the sword with me. A draft of stagnant air came from the top of a rickety staircase.

The door behind me rattled shut and vanished. The only way left was up.

My heart pounded in my chest. An unconvincing voice in my head whispered that this could be the way to Emmet.

I started climbing. At the top, I pressed my hand against the low ceiling to avoid hitting my head. I entered a large attic with hardwood flooring and a sloped wood ceiling. An oil lamp burned atop a table, old maps and star charts decorating the walls.

A man's broad back greeted me, bent over an open book on the table.

He glanced at me over his shoulder and straightened his body. He was tall and sturdily built, with raven hair and a beard peppered with gray. Thick eyebrows covered his smoky eyes. He wore a whitecoat over a dark shirt and darker pants. A sword shone silver in his hand.

"Welcome, witch. I've been waiting on you."

He charged me, eyes arrogant and cruel, sword poised to kill. I hit him with a ball of energy. He came to a halt. My magic fizzed and fell at his feet.

Shit, only Immortals can neutralize magic like that.

The blade in my hand turned green. The color of fear. "Feast on it," I whispered to the sword as the Immortal came at me again.

His blade thrust and I dodged. I spun quickly and our swords connected. Pain shot through my arm. My opponent had beastly strength. He leapt back and I charged. He waited for me only to slide away right before my blade found his flesh. The stranger grabbed my shoulder, forced me to face him and ran his blade clean through my stomach.

My whole body erupted in pain as my flesh tore open.

An Immortal swordsman versus me. Could I expect any better?

The Immortal pulled me onto my feet by my hair.

A stern voice boomed out. "Dimitri!"

Winter snapped his fingers and a levitation force lifted the bloodthirsty Immortal off the floor, pinning him against the ceiling.

Dimitri belly-laughed. "Brother, you brought the witchling. Good."

What's he saying?

Winter released him and Dimitri's body plunged to the floor.

"What is the meaning of this, Dimitri?" Winter asked. "You are not a witch hunter."

Dimitri rubbed his beard. "The Grand Magistrate foresaw that you would be instrumental in guiding the girl to the Sacred Vault. He assigned me the task of finding out what she is and why you have shown an interest."

"The Grand Magistrate set you on this course?" Winter said.

Denial much, Winter?

"Yeah, who else?" Dimitri said, put off. "I've just told you that."

"And this whole charade?" Winter asked.

Dimitri nodded. "My masterstroke. Simply taking the girl wouldn't shed as much light as watching how she'd fight through hellacious odds under your tutelage to save her wolf lover. We wanted to see her take a few blows. A test drive if you don't mind the metaphor."

"No one's driving me," I hissed at the prick.

He grinned. "She's got spirit, brother, did you give her a bend yet?"

I raised my hands which were already glowing purple.

Dimitri laughed harder and stepped back in mock surrender.

Winter pushed my hands down gently.

"Take it easy with the jokes," Winter threatened.

"Forgive me, spirited wench," Dimitri said as he bowed. "I do not live in your modern world."

Still offensive, you creep!

Dimitri cleared his throat. "Our Wise Master wanted me to assure you, Chief Magistrate Winter, he only wants the young witch. You have nothing to fear from the Council. You played the part Düsternis foresaw to perfection. In fact, the old Seventh is more than grateful to you, boyo, for locating this freakish anomaly of a witch and leading her right to us."

Düsternis had sensed all along there was more to me than met the eye. The Grand Magistrate was nearly as powerful as an Eternal. Winter's cloaking of my etheric essence was ill conceived.

There I go again, trusting a man.

Winter raised his hands to shoulder height, palms up. A tremendous energy field shot out and ensnared Dimitri, thrusting him against the wall.

The attic walls shook and hummed amidst the intense energy wave.

Dimitri went pale. He struggled to speak, as Winter's magic clamped onto his throat. "You can't use Shadow force on a Magistrate of the Council."

Winter's face went completely savage. "Yet, it's happening."

"The Council and the Umbra Order will not stand for

this. You will bear the consequences."

I cringed as the magistrate choked and clawed at his own throat as Winter increased the pressure. "And who will tell them?" he asked Dimitri, raising an eyebrow. "You?"

Dimitri's face burned with anger as it dawned on him. "You, a Chief Magistrate and Iron Warrior of the First Umbra Order, would kill a magistrate of the Seventh Council to keep this puny girl from your own Master? Does honor mean nothing to you?"

Yes, he would. That was slowly dawning on me, too.

A ghastly roar burst from Winter's throat. Electricity buzzed over my skin, making me shudder. He launched a wave of energy that hit the back wall, demolishing it as if it were made of paper. Rocketing debris, dust and whole chunks of wall hit me everywhere. I coughed. The wound in my stomach throbbed with pain.

Dimitri twisted his body—his muscles strained to fight off Winter's hold on him in vain.

Winter paced back and forth like a caged animal. He banged his free fist against the wall. I saw through his anguish. He didn't want to do what he was about to do, but he saw no other choice.

The words kept spinning in my head.

He doesn't want to kill him, but he will... for me.

Dimitri grunted. "Do this and you'll forfeit your very etheric essence."

Winter nodded, slowly. "I know."

"Winter," I said, "we can find—"

Suddenly, faster than I could finish my sentence, Winter stuck two fingers inside Dimitri's eyes, blinding him. The magistrate's face contorted. His body warped out of control. His screams shuddered me to my core.

Dimitri's life force and immortal essence spilled out of him like waves of steam and light, rippling across the room. The energy hit me like a ton of bricks, knocking me back onto the floor. Claws scratched my insides and nipped at my heart. I felt powerless, overrun by the colossal wave.

If this is what Shadows can do to other Immortals, why have I been so stupid as to hang out not with one but two of them?

Winter shook, phosphorescent energy entering him from every pore. His skin became translucent as he absorbed the magistrate's etheric essence, something I didn't think possible.

Dimitri's body slid to the floor, lifeless.

Winter grabbed Dimitri by the hair, lifting his head off the floor. His hand burst through Dimitri's chest, snatching out the heart.

Again, I had to fight not to vomit.

Flames ignited around the heart, still in Winter's hand, lighting it up.

I was stunned and out of words, my sword at the other side of the room glowing with a bright, alarming green.

Winter fell to his knees, wiped out.

I had no idea what to tell him or if I should talk at all. The words fell out of my mouth in a daze. "I don't know what to say. Thank you, I guess. That must have been hard."

His eyes had no life left in them as he hooked them on mine. "Hard? I killed Dimitri. I killed an old spirit and a friend. And why? For doing his job, for following orders."

He roared out that ghastly scream again. I covered my ears.

It was excruciating just to climb to my feet. The room spun out of control, and I grabbed onto a reading table to keep from falling.

Dragging my feet, I made my way to the staircase. In his fury, Winter had killed the one person who could tell us where they had Emmet and I just stood by, watching, saying too little, too late.

Emmet must be somewhere in the vault. So be it. I'd find him myself.

Winter opened his hand to toss a luminescent current of energy in my path to block my access to the staircase.

"Stay," he said.

"I have to find Emmet," I said through clenched teeth.

Almost as important, I wanted to get away from Winter. Shadow Warriors scared the shit out of me. Way too hardcore. I fought against his energy, but all I had left was pain.

Boots on the staircase, moving fast as if leaping three steps at a time.

Chaos. Even *his* jaw dropped when he spotted Dimitri's remains.

He glanced at me tenderly and poked at Winter's field.

"What deeds most dastardly have I laid mine two eyes upon?"

The current hissed and faded away.

Chaos stared at Dimitri's lifeless body. For an instant, I saw a true curiosity in his expression, a feeling most rare for Immortals.

"Tsk, tsk, I would have done it for you, old friend," he told Winter. "We'd have less mess to clean."

Winter's eyes were murderous. "What do you want?"

Chaos shrugged. "You know, I did clean up more untidiness you left strewn throughout the corridors. In addition, I killed a bunch of unsightly creatures who would have become quite the gossips if left unattended to. Not a big whoop, but appreciation would be more warranted than vitriol."

I sat down, feeling weaker by the second.

A troglodyte scuttled into the attic. Chaos twirled his finger, snapping the troglodyte's neck. "You see," Chaos said casually, "I am nothing if not a team player, handling all the ugly little details overlooked by others."

His smile did a one-eighty when he saw I wasn't moving on the floor.

Chaos furrowed his brow. "Why is the girl not healing?"

Winter's eyes widened as he looked my way. Blood pooled beneath me—my stomach, where I'd been stabbed, ached like hell at the slightest touch.

A jaw muscle twitched in Winter's face. "I don't know."

The two Shadows rushed to my side, kneeling down.

What could they do? They caused wounds, not healed them.

Winter grabbed my mutilated thermal shirt and ripped it off my body.

"What the hell are you doing?" I said, slurring the words.

He ripped my leggings off, too, leaving me in my bra and panties, both saturated in my own blood.

How embarrassing to be half-naked in front of the men who were the very bane of my existence. Maybe the gaping hole in my midsection would keep their eyes off the rest of my body.

They've probably seen it all before anyway, a few thousand times.

"If I'm not healing," I said, "does that mean I'll die?"

Winter's face was at best ambivalent. "Think back," he said. "Did anything strange happen since we entered the vault?"

I shook my head. "I don't know. Seeing that everything is always strange since I met you two nightmares, it's hard to choose."

"Try," Winter implored.

"Okay, well, I felt that sharp pinch in the dark."

Chaos's hands were all over me, searching my ribcage. I tried to kick him but could barely lift my foot off the ground.

He found something and with his thumb and forefinger

quickly pinched it—*and me*—so damn hard. I doubled over in pain and tried to push his hand away.

Winter grabbed my hands and forced me back down.

"Assholes!" I moaned.

Chaos extracted a thin, gold needle from my flesh.

"Bonshek," Winter said. "It slows cell regeneration down to a drip."

"Will I die?" I said.

Chaos dropped the needle. "It wouldn't have taken down someone as old as Winter or yours truly, but with you—"

He stopped talking.

This bonshek thingy must be very, very bad.

"It's very rare magic," Winter said, "and probably what they aimed for all along. It's why we were led to the vault."

"Idiots, will I die or not?"

"You'll live, as long as you stay with me," Chaos said with a wink. "Look what already happened with this other one."

"Okay," I said. "I don't get it. They had to drag me all the way to Alaska to stick a needle in me?"

"Bonshek only works in high magic zones, like Serenity Valley and the Vault," Winter said. "Places that expand and carry magic on their own. Having you here was the only way to put you to the test."

"We can assume the council knows I can't die."

Winter gave it some thought. "They couldn't be sure."

"And now that my impetuous friend Frosty has vanquished poor Dimitri," Chaos added, "they may remain in the dark, but their suspicion level will have reached code Orange."

"It's fricking cold in here," I said. "My toes are like ice cubes."

"She may be worse than I thought," Chaos said. "I'm afraid our little pumpkin will bleed out faster than she can heal."

The fuck?

Winter flared his nostrils. "She'll need Immortal blood," he said, hooking onto Chaos's mad eyes. "A lot of it."

Chaos frowned. "I didn't sign on for this," he said, pouting. He flexed his arm and tapped a bulging vein. "This blood is 100% immortal octane. I can't just dispense it to anyone."

Winter drew out a dagger from his boot and slashed open Chaos's arm.

"Why him?" I protested, squirming. "I don't want madman blood."

Chaos stretched his arm over my stomach, letting the blood spill into my stab wound. Every time his arm healed Winter had to reopen the vein.

His blood warmed my shivering body. I closed my eyes, fading in and out for a while before I felt my magic spreading to my nerves like warm milk, releasing all tension. I could breathe again.

When I regained full consciousness, the world had stopped spinning. The bleeding gush had vanished and been replaced by pink, delicate skin.

Now Winter slashed my wrist with his dagger, then did the same to Chaos. I watched our wrists bond through the exchange of our blood.

My body fed hungrily on Chaos's Immortal red cells.

"Are we wrist vampires now?" I joked.

"Good, her sense of humor is back," Winter said.

"That was a sense of humor?" Chaos said, perplexed.

Winter grinned at me. "What passes for one."

Great. The two Immortal morons amused each other.

I knew I was healed because I found them annoying again.

I grabbed Winter's hand. "You didn't answer me. Why his blood? Why not you? Why not your blood, Winter?"

"We used the strongest blood," he said, wrapping me in his sweater.

Chapter 22

THE DOOR TO THE archives was unremarkable compared to the warded, massive wooden double doors of the greater library. A small, white door with a floral pattern around the frame and a brass handle.

"Are the protective fields disarmed?" Chaos said.

Winter nodded.

Chaos opened the door with a flick of his wrist. We entered a rectangular room narrowed by the shelves that lined the walls all the way to the ceiling. The middle shelves were occupied with thick file folders, but the top and bottom shelves were all but empty.

"Is this all there is?" I said.

Honestly, I'd expected there'd be a lot more files.

"We Immortals are limited in numbers," Chaos said. "We don't squeeze out offspring willy-nilly every time we get soused. Our power lies in the strength of the individual."

Yeah, okay, I get the point.

We passed through the archives to another white door and then descended a winding staircase. The staircase brought us to a humid room with grungy brick walls and cement support columns. The floor was dirty. Arctic cold air blew out of ceiling vents. This wasn't a room—it was a cell.

There was a cough. We looked to each other. Not us.

The cough again. We all spotted a small mound of rags in the corner.

"Emmet!" I yelled and ran to him.

We pulled off the rags and found him shackled to a chain that was fastened to the wall above him. Winter lifted him to a seated position. Emmet could not lift his hanging head. His knuckles were bruised as if he had been punching the wall. He had lost a ton of weight. His ribs protruded out of his torn shirt. His arms were covered with cuts, bruises and burns.

"Emmet," I repeated as I bent down to lift his head and look into his vacant eyes. I kissed his bruised and battered face. I tried to hug him, but he moaned at the slightest touch. I kissed him again, stroking his hair.

His eyelids fluttered.

"Yes," I said. "You can do it. Come back to me, Emmet."

He squinted at me through swollen eyelids. "Is this heaven?" he muttered through dry lips. "Are you an angel?"

Chaos snorted behind me.

"It's me... Sophie," I said, smiling through my tears.

He leaned closer, trying to comprehend. "You shouldn't be here."

"I'm here to take you home," I said, stroking his face.

He still didn't understand. "It's only a dream. I've been sleeping."

I looked up to Winter. He had his arms crossed, not moving a muscle. A shadow shivered in his eyes.

"Do something about the shackles, yeah?" I told him.

"The shackles are the least of wolfie's problems," Chaos said. "There are bruises days old on him. He's not healing."

It was true. Shifters didn't have the same infinite capacity for regeneration as Immortals, but they were strong and healed much faster than basic humans. Emmet's body should be able to clear bruises in a day or two.

"What's happening?" I said.

"His ribs," Winter said, kneeling next to me.

I felt Emmet's skin under his torn shirt. I touched something cold protruding out of his left side. Emmet winced. I found the same thing on the right side, underneath his ribcage.

"Is it bonshek?" I said.

Winter nodded. "They used a huge amount on him to not only make sure he wouldn't heal but more importantly that he wouldn't shift."

Chaos yawned. "Tell me we're leaving him to die. His life is so pointlessly short anyway."

I felt tempted to tell him to go to hell, but I knew he liked to say those things more than he believed them. He also saved my life not long ago.

Winter tore the bloodied shirt off Emmet and clutched onto one of the metal rods, dragging it out. A deep growl rolled out of Emmet. I held him tight, whispering *it's going to be okay* in his ear over and over.

Winter pulled out the second rod and dropped both on the ground.

I looked at the rods that had prevented Emmet from shifting. I had been stabbed with a thin needle, but these things were three inches long and thick as nails. I couldn't imagine how much they must have damaged him. At least, he hadn't taken a sword to the gut and his wounds would probably heal on their own now, without the boost of potent blood.

Winter broke the shackles around Emmet's wrists with his bare hands.

I fell into Emmet's arms, hugging him tight enough that he cringed. The worst was behind us—Emmet was alive, his body felt warm and would start healing soon, and he had finally found enough strength to hug me back.

"Sophie," he said. "Is that really you?"

"It's me," I told him, but was overcome with guilt and regret. "We're going to get you out of here, okay?"

Emmet lifted his head. I finally looked into his eyes. Gone was the usual hint of mirth and mischief in those hazel eyes of his, that had always been there no matter what was happening. "I need to heal," he said.

"You can do that at home," I said, my voice breaking.

"He needs to shift to accelerate his healing," Chaos informed me. "Let him do his tail wagging while we tie up our final loose ends."

Emmet released my hand. His body shook and lurched. His skin cracked and white fur spurted forth. His ears elongated, a snout spilling out where his nose used to be. When the transformation was complete, a majestic white wolf was crouching next to me, his ears pointed. The wolf was over five feet tall, standing on powerful legs. Red patches of blood spotted his soft white fur.

Even in his animal form, Emmet was magnificent.

The wolf sat down to rest and licked his paws. Winter gently nudged me toward the stairs. We went past the archives and back to the library.

"Okay, now what?" I said.

"Every trace of you having been here must be erased," Chaos said. He glanced at Winter. "You too, *magistrado*. Düsternis will know something is up. He's a fucking twat, but he's not stupid. He'll figure out your involvement."

Winter shook his head. "I can handle Düsternis."

"No, Sir Galahad, you can't."

Fearing another argument was about to start, I stepped between them.

"How do we destroy the evidence?" I asked.

"I've already interlaced crisscrossing beams, tying them to

the four main foundational points outside, cutting off the vault's reverberations," Chaos said, "and Old Man Winter here has done a decent job of blocking all transmitting signals on the inside." His face contorted at having just paid Winter even a half-assed compliment.

"You said yourself that Düsternis is no idiot," I reminded Chaos. "Even if there's no proof Winter and I were ever here, how long before he makes an educated guess? I mean, who else could have done this? We broke into the impenetrable fortress known as Sacred Vault, slaughtered half the guards, killed an Immortal magistrate and freed a prisoner."

Chaos flashed his wicked grin. "It is I who could have done it. And by the time I'm done, *all* guards will be slaughtered."

I chewed on that for a while. Winter's face was unreadable.

"Am I hearing this right, Chaos?" I said. "You'll take the blame?"

Chaos grinned. "It's not like Düsternis can like me any less."

"Maybe it doesn't matter? You and Winter worked really hard to isolate the vault from the outer world."

"That won't last forever. As soon as we're gone, the shields will weaken, and the vault's channels will reopen eventually. The only solution, sugar pop, is that we make it look like I raided the vault and destroyed the archives."

Winter raised an eyebrow. "The archives?"

"That's key, old chum," Chaos explained with pride. "No one will suspect the world's oldest boy scout of incinerating the hallowed archives. That reminds me, if there's anything in there that you need, you know, for future witch stalking purposes, or whatever, I suggest you grab it now."

Winter's features turned as rigid as a mask. "The archives are of immeasurable value. It's not just Immortals, the world's history—the world's true history, not the one recorded by the victors—is in there."

Chaos gave me an *I-told-you* look. "The good magistrate has just illustrated my point. Burning the archives is a necessity."

"If you destroy the archives, all eternal and immortal councils will want a piece of you," Winter pushed back. "There will be no force in any of the realms that could convince them to change their minds. You will be the most hunted man in the history of the world."

"Has a nice ring to it," Chaos gloated. He drew his Damascus sword out of its sheath. A soft white light flared about him like a magic cloak. His dark aura shimmered. My skin prickled.

"I already killed anyone I could find along the river," he said.

"It was you?" I said. "You killed those troglodytes by the river?"

He nodded, manic grin on his face.

"Why did you have to make it so brutal?"

"Why do you think, sugar plum?" he said. "To throw the council off your scent and to remind those buffoons I know all their secrets."

Okay, yeah, Chaos knew about the experiments at the Palacio and beyond. Winter had explained how he had gotten the power of the third-eye vision from Horror, like his brain could connect to the Eternal network at any time. Beyond creepy.

I saw the reflection of his face in his blade. An electric shock hit my heart. A primeval connection buzzed inside my chest, pulling me to Chaos like all reason had escaped me. Was it because his blood was in my veins now? No, I remembered that I had the same feeling when I saw him draw that sword in that first battle in Serenity Valley.

Chaos raised the sword above his head. The sword came down, slashing at the air. The blade whizzed and flashed a dark brown—the color of hate.

I stepped back, feeling lightheaded, and bumped into Winter's chest.

"Is he going to murder all those troglodytes in cold blood?" I said. "They didn't want to hurt me."

"They didn't want to fight you," Winter said. "There's a difference."

"Those fiends have come through the Eternal gates," Chaos said. "They are not what they seem to be. Have you heard of Horror, sweet thing?"

I nodded. "One of the first Eternals."

"Smart girl. Düsternis has been chatting up Horror," he said as he kept swinging his blade.

Winter grasped Chaos's sword hand. "What do you mean?"

The ground beneath my feet felt shaky. "Horror isn't the only Eternal," I interjected. "It could be someone else who's orchestrated this."

Chaos lowered the sword. "It is him. I sense him. His etheric essence floats in this very library. It bounces off the backs of the dwarf beasts." He looked at me, curiously. "You don't seem surprised I feel his presence, Luna."

I met his gaze. "Winter told me all about you and Horror."

Chaos inhaled, stepped back, and raised an eyebrow at Winter.

"What?" I said, sensing a sudden uneasiness.

Winter said nothing. He was very good at hiding his emotions, but his eyes, dark and troubled, betrayed him.

I knew they were hiding something.

Winter stepped closer and took my hand. "It's imperative that we sanitize the scene, that we leave no evidence behind. Horror must never see you, he must never hear of you, he must never smell you. Do you understand? He must never know of you, Luna. His power is as old as the magic realm itself. You cannot win once he reclaims it. Nobody can."

The lord of the soul swallowers. Was it Horror?

My heartbeat slowed. The breath in my lungs felt heavy. Pushing the words out of my mouth made me dizzy. "Isn't he confined to his eternal chambers, his access to the magic realm cut off?"

"As far as we know, yes," Winter said.

Chaos kept silent. He licked his lips and I saw it, shining through layers and layers of badassery in his eyes. The bleak shadow warrior felt fear. I couldn't understand at first why he had warned us of the vault, or why he had followed us to make sure we'd succeed in getting Emmet and walking out without leaving evidence, but now it made sense.

If Horror returned to the world, it meant Chaos would be in far greater danger than he was pissing Düsternis off. He needed my help. No army of rogue Immortals would stand by him in a showdown with Horror, but maybe all he needed to have a glimmer of hope was the ethereal power of a mist rider.

Chaos quickly shook the trepidation off his face. "How about we get this show on the road?" he said. He spun around, holding his sword in front of his face. "Where art thou, my little uglies?"

A wave of magic erupted from him and I felt it all the way down to my fingertips. It was sharp, high-energy magic that made me giddy as I drank it in.

The ground shook with the thundering echoes of hundreds of boots marching. Packs of troglodytes, dwarves and huge black dogs swarmed the library, summoned by Chaos and his sword.

Bloodlust and impatience shone across their bare teeth. The Vault guards, the ones who came straight through the gates of hell according to Chaos, were intoxicated by the dense magic and had begun to abandon all reason.

Chaos licked the shimmering Damascus blade in his hand. "I can't control every single one of your minds, my pretties, so you'll have to taste my thousand-year-old steel."

His sword glowed above his head before he brought it down, slaughtering two troglodytes who charged him.

Axes and spears thrust and whipped. Chaos screamed so loud my ears popped. He sliced and cut through flesh like a man possessed, not caring about the multitude of wounds he incurred.

The creatures kept coming. I watched Chaos's wrath and became hypnotized by his flowing movements.

Winter flew past, sword blazing in his hand. He kicked a dwarf that got in his way and sent him bounding off into the air like he was a football, then banged two more dwarf heads together.

As more beasts rushed into the library, drawn to Chaos's summoning power, Winter joined the furor of slaughter, his sword chopping to pieces any beast in his vicinity. Heads and limbs went flying in a bloodbath that was all too reminiscent of the metamorphic night.

I bent over, sick to my stomach. Sharp magic bit my tongue. Two shadows fighting side by side—it was just too much carnage. I closed my eyes.

"Halt!" Chaos barked out.

I opened my eyes. All creatures but three had been slaughtered, most quartered or at least beheaded. A stream of dark crimson blood flowed beneath the piles of bodies that covered the marble floor completely.

Winter's face and hair glistened with sweat as he continued to breathe heavily from the extreme exercise of slaughter.

Chaos extended two bloodied arms, inviting the creatures, two troglodytes and one dwarf, over to him.

"Come forth, hounds of hell," he told them. "You have a very important mission to fulfill."

Guttural cries answered his command. There was no intelligence left in the beasts. They knelt in front of Chaos. He touched their heads one by one and murmured in a language I didn't understand.

Winter glided to my side. "He is imprinting memories," he explained. "When he's done, they'll only have memories of Chaos in the vault, so when their master finds them, they will report back it was Chaos who caused the mayhem all by himself."

Chaos stepped back. The troglodytes and the dwarf gazed upon him as if he were a deity before they ran off.

"I'm done with the dummies," he said. "Now let's burn all the Loony Luna evidence to the ground."

The two Immortals gingerly stepped over bodies on the way to the attic staircase.

"Are you coming?" Winter asked me.

I shook my head. "I'd just be in the way."

As soon as they left, I slipped away to the archive room. Chaos had suggested that we take anything we wanted.

I didn't have much time. Of all the possibilities, I had to pick one fast. The ceiling-high shelves that held thousands of file folders rose above my head.

How could I get the file I wanted before Winter and Chaos returned?

His sweater. It was the only piece of clothing I had since Dimitri stabbed me in the attic and my clothes were ripped off me.

I took Winter's sweater off and stood in my underwear. I balled it up and brought it to my face to inhale his etheric essence. My magic grabbed onto the essence as it filled my nose. A folder shuddered up on the shelves. I stood on tiptoes and strained my spine to get to it. Winter's file.

I leafed through pages written in foreign languages, Latin and Greek and Norse and Chinese, all languages I couldn't read. I finally found a handful of pages in English and quickly scanned through them.

My heart pounded as I read, a heavy weight pressing down on my chest. The room shrank. I felt helpless, holding back tears that had been gathering for days.

Footsteps approached. I tore the few pages in English off the file folder and returned it to the shelf, quickly putting the sweater back on.

Winter looked me over slowly. My cheeks were on fire, I could feel it.

"Everything is clean in the attic," he said. "It now looks like Chaos killed Dimitri. His essence is the only thing left in the library."

I nodded. "That's good, right?"

Chaos burst through the door holding a box of matches. "We'll do this the old-fashioned way," he said, manic grin on his face.

Winter glanced up and down the shelves. His eyes looked like the loneliest northern sea, eternal sadness sinking deep. "Do it," he said.

Chaos struck a match. "Time to set the world on fire."

Chapter 23

I STARED AT THE phone after Emmet hung up. It had been two days since our return, and he assured me he was healing fast. Two broken ribs and his sprained wrist were much improved but not quite a hundred percent.

He wasn't in any pain, that was the important part.

Emmet stayed with his dad who had twice asked to be put on the phone to express his gratitude to me.

The violent memories of his ordeal at the vault still rattled Emmet.

How could they not?

He never once asked me how I found out where he had been taken, or how I had enlisted two Immortals to help. After an awkward silence, Emmet thanked me again and told me he had to go.

I wouldn't blame him if he never wanted to see me again.

He must have realized by now just how dangerous being close to me could be.

Lucia's sunroom was getting chilly. The evening sky was overcast. A thunder sounded off in the distance.

What I had glimpsed about Winter's life at the vault weighed heavily on my mind. I wanted to know more—perhaps if I learned about the man who had watched me since birth and urged me to take destiny into my own hands, it would help me understand both his motivations and my reality better.

The pages I had stolen were sitting in my purse. I had sneaked them out of the vault tucked inside my bra. I feared Winter would bust me, or that the pages themselves wouldn't withstand the turbulence of the ley line express, but they had made it out intact.

I tapped my fingernails on the windowpane.

What to do?

I was ready. I opened the purse and touched my fingers to the edge of those folded pages. I let the pages go for a moment and then I gripped onto them, pulling them out.

Sitting on the couch, I straightened my pleated skirt and unfolded the creased pages. As if licked by flames, the pages began to shrink, all four corners shriveling up until all that was left in my lap were ashes.

I watched, stunned, as the ashes evaporated into the ether. It was as if the pages had never existed. They were infused with a vanishing spell.

The Immortal files held mysteries never meant to be removed from the archives—never intended for curious outsiders. It was probably the reason why no copies were kept.

I closed my eyes, recalling all that I had retained from that quick glimpse inside the Sacred Vault archive room.

Winter was born during the Nordic bronze era in 1231 BC which made him over 3,200 years old. That number alone should have given me pause and a good reason to stay away from him. His birthplace was what is known as the Trondheim Fjord in modern day Norway. He had become a Viking around the 9th century AD and he had been a king, a general and a priest to the Norse god Vidar, probably not in that order. He had left Scandinavia many times for the Mediterranean Sea area, especially ancient Greece. There wasn't any information on his parents in the file except for a numeric reference to their separate files.

The only mention of Chaos that I spotted as I scanned the pages was an event around 913 AD when Winter and Chaos helped save a Chinese village from starvation by introducing new agriculture methods. I'd found nothing about how or when they became shadows.

The thing that had given me pause, though, and had haunted me ever since I read it, was the child that Winter had fathered with a basic woman named Helen Ashford, as recently as 1954. According to the file, that was the only child Winter ever had. Both mother and baby boy were killed in a car crash in early 1955.

Children born of Immortals and basic parents didn't fully grow into their immortality until they reached adolescence after the Immortal parent kickstarted their etheric essence. Winter's son never made it to that stage.

The file stated that the Seventh Council had issued a warning that the chief magistrate and shadow warrior was grieving, and that grief had made him unreliable. They suggested giving him a decade before approaching him with any council related matters.

That was where I had stopped reading, interrupted by the return of Winter and Chaos, but I yearned to find out more.

Winter had lost his one and only child, a baby boy named Christian. He had mated with a basic woman. His grief had lasted for at least a decade. He had lied when he said he had never experienced fatherly love. Maybe that pain of loss still lingered.

Everything I thought I knew about him collapsed and went up in flames. There was a part of him that was very human and vulnerable. I didn't know what to do with that information. I could never ask him about it, and he would never answer. Of that, I was certain.

My phone rang, startling me.

"*It's over,*" Faion yelled into the receiver, blasting my eardrum. "*The troglodyte elite fighting force have retreated to the mountains as our own troglodytes handed them their asses.*"

I took a deep breath in. "For now," I said. "That's great

news, but it's not over. I'm not sure anything ever ends."

I didn't know if he had heard me. *"Our Tam girl is fierce, I'm telling you,"* he went on. *"She fought with them troglos and taught them a thing or two."*

I smiled. "I can't wait to see you both."

"Day after tomorrow," Faion said. *"At my crib."*

Whatever Chaos had done had worked. Somehow, he had singlehandedly solved every single one of my problems and then vanished, leaving no trace. And now his blood was running in my veins and I owed him my life.

Not how I thought things would go. Strange bedfellows as they say.

"Sophie, Lily, dinner's ready," Lucia called from the kitchen. To my great relief, she was doing well, she seemed happy and well-adjusted to her everyday life.

The red wine beef stew was steaming in the ceramic pot. Lily set the table and I reached for some paper napkins. Lightning cut the evening sky in half. I looked out the window and froze in place like a dangling icicle.

Winter was crouched on the tile roof of the house across the street. A second lightning flashed behind him, turning his eyes a red gold. I caught a glimpse of his teeth as he grinned and then leapt off to the neighboring roof.

He stood up as raindrops started falling, his blond hair caught in the sparse moonlight. He looked like an ancient savage deity, elegant and frightening, stirring awe and fear in the souls of his subjects.

Oh god. I drew the blinds shut.

"I can't stay for dinner, sorry, Lucia," I said as I dashed to the door.

"What?" Lily said. "That stew is Lucia's masterwork."

"Save some for me," I yelled, yanking the front door open.

"Here," Lucia said, tossing me her red umbrella. "Don't stay out too late."

"Mom, what the hell?" I heard Lily's voice as I slammed the door shut.

My eyes darted up the line of roofs across the street, past satellite antennae and downspouts, looking for Winter.

A dull thud echoed behind me. I spun around as Winter landed in a soft crouch, glossy droplets sparkling on his smiling face.

"What are you doing?" I said.

"Waiting for you," he said. "And watching the neighborhood to make sure no foul beasts lurk in the shadows."

"And? Did you find any?"

He shook his head. "Besides you? None."

Raindrops lashed my face. I opened Lucia's umbrella.

"Is it really over?" I said.

"It will never be over, Luna, not while Horror breathes, but this part has concluded. Düsternis called off the search for you, rattled at the death of an Immortal Magistrate and the incineration of the archives."

"He now wants Chaos more than he wants me," I concluded.

"Yes. Much more."

"I can't say I blame him."

The air was lush. His hair was wet down to his scalp, but I didn't think it bothered him one bit. He reveled in the water elements of the cold season.

"Will you come with me?" he said.

"To the condo?"

"No, you'll see."

Fifteen minutes later, we walked through my apartment door. It took me more than a moment to catch my breath. Everything was clean and neatly organized like never before. The walls were restored and painted a soft pistachio color, an expensive Persian rug unfolded under a cherry wood coffee table, a velvety chocolate couch was still in its wrap, the cupboards were painted a deep burgundy with brass handles, and the bookshelves... the bookshelves were lined with my books, many of which were replaced with identical copies.

"I don't know what to say. Thank you, Jonas, but you didn't have to do all this. I won't be staying here long."

"The least I could do," he said. "And maybe you'll reconsider leaving. In any case, I paid your lease up front for a year. This place will be waiting for your return even if you go."

I stared at him, more and more perplexed as the seconds passed.

"You're mad at me," he said. "You think I overstepped."

"No. I just don't know what to make of you."

He passed his hand over his wet blond hair made spikey by

rain and humidity. "That's okay. I don't know what to make of me either."

The pantry had been completely stocked. I smiled as I appreciated every single item before I took out a box of black chai.

"Would you like some tea?" I asked Winter.

"Yeah, that sounds good."

I poured Evian water into two cups and set the microwave timer.

"By the way, I told the police I'd asked you to keep an eye on my apartment," I said. "You're off the suspect list."

"That's good to know."

I opened the breadbox which contained two loaves of bakery bread.

The microwave buzzer meant the water was ready. I plopped the tea bags in the cups and handed one to Winter.

"*Merci*, Sophie," he said.

"This is so civilized," I said as we were about to have tea for two.

"You don't think me capable of civility," he said, arching an eyebrow.

"You can be a total brute at times."

"Dimitri," he said, becoming somber. "I lost my temper after that. I'm truly sorry. None of that was your fault."

I nodded, not wanting to talk about those things.

We sipped our chai latte. The silence hung between us.

He set his cup down and gazed into my eyes. "Luna, I can

agree that Chaos came through for us. You must never forget that he can turn on you faster than you can spell *boo*. His agenda, if he even knows it, is so convoluted, so misguided and self-centered that you could never even hope to guess and if you did, it would change the very next day. Trust me, I learned the hard way."

"He was your friend."

Winter rubbed his chin. "I was his mentor."

My jaw dropped so hard I had to push it back up.

"At the Umbra Order after he escaped Horror. I helped him become a Shadow Warrior. In part, I am responsible for what he's become."

It was all beginning to make some sense. "The student spurns the teacher?"

"Like I said, his reasons, his causes, are too convoluted to make any sense of them outside of his own twisted mind."

"Why did you help him?"

"I thought he could change, but his damage is too deep."

I nodded.

"He will come back for you and when it happens, I'd like to be close."

A cold shiver ran down the length of my spine. The certainty of his prediction was hard to refute.

"I get it, Jonas, but I can't let Chaos or Horror or Düsternis dictate my life."

"Or me," he said, pensively. "I get it."

"Yes, but that's beside the point. If I hide, if I stop living my life the way I want, then they win already, and I cease to be me."

"I'm going to tell you a final thing and then go. I see the unconquerable spirit in you, and I respect it. Despite my brusque manner, I would not bother if I did not think you worth the trouble."

I didn't know what to say.

He got up and glanced about the room proudly. "You have terrible taste in furniture," he said. "I hope you enjoy the new décor."

"Jonas, stay."

Am I losing my mind?

He furrowed his brow. "Are you sure?"

"No, I'm not."

He stroked my cheek, his fingers sliding into my hair, pulling my head back to expose my neck.

"I'm not a gentle man."

"Of that, I'm sure."

He locked his fingers with mine and pulled me to my feet. Our eyes locked for a few excruciating seconds and then his lips crushed on mine.

I felt shaken to my core, unable to respond to his kiss, my arms dangling at my sides, helplessly.

His tongue pressed my lips open, searching for my tongue. *Oh.My.God.* Nothing tasted better than him. He was sweet and sour, lemon popsicles and chocolate fudge. He was a feast for all senses.

I threw my arms around his neck, standing on tiptoes. Was this another goodbye kiss? If so, it was pretty spectacular—and necessary.

Before I had a chance to fully absorb what was going on, he lifted me up, hands under my butt. My breath caught in my throat and I was left with my senses spinning.

I pushed against his chest and then got myself wrapped around him, pulling him closer. I pushed him away and then pulled him close, then pushed him away again.

"You're nuts," he said. "I like it."

I opened my mouth for a snappy response, but he kissed me quiet.

What am I doing?

There was no way I could handle this man. I could draw chunks of energy from the moon and I could take castles down, but what did I know about making love to a Shadow?

Could I rule out he wasn't working on his agenda still, perhaps without even realizing it? He was probably doing his best to keep me in San Diego and for a moment or two I fell for it, and why? Because he had mesmerizing eyes and a hypnotizing voice? Because every pore on his skin screamed strength? What about his grief over his child? Was that over? What were sixty-five years to a three-thousand-year-old man? Sixty-five years was like yesterday to him. Could I handle his temper? His violence? Was I ready for any of that?

No, of course not, this was all kinds of wrong.

"Winter," I said, breathless. "This is too much too fast."

He dropped his head, held on for a moment and then released me with a growl. "Did I do something wrong?"

I shook my head. "It's all too much, you know?"

"I can stay to watch over you," he said. "I can sleep on the couch."

That would be a terrible idea. The whole world was still spinning on its axis, my fingers aching to touch him again.

"I need time to process everything," I said. "Touch base tomorrow?"

He nodded, kissed my hand and vanished into the rain.

Chapter 24

GRAM SET HER SUITCASE down. She took in every detail of the neatly organized studio apartment.

"Sophie, your place looks wonderful, so cozy and inviting. You've done a great job, sweetie."

If only, Gram. I took her coat to hang in the closet.

"So, next Wednesday is the big day," she said. "Wish we had more time."

"Thursday," I corrected her. "Two o'clock in the afternoon."

"That's good. You'll have the morning to get ready for your flight."

I set a plate of cookies and pastries out with a jug of lemon iced tea.

"I have someone here I think you'd like to see," Gram said.

She unzipped her handbag. Nanya lifted her little head slowly out of the bag and then leapt off onto Gram's lap.

"You brought the borgo?" I said, not quite believing my eyes.

"The word was she missed me and I missed the little fluff, too. I thought we deserved a trip together."

I petted Nanya under the chin. She loved that. She stretched her tiny legs and rolled onto her back, granting me access to her belly.

"Look at that," Gram said. "She knows you."

"Of course she does, I took her home, remember?"

Gram smiled happily. "Will you visit for Easter, Sophie?"

"We'll see, Gram. I'll do my best."

"Don't forget to pack warm clothes, honey."

Gram's mother hen instincts were out in full force.

I grinned. "No, Gram, I'll just take my tank tops and bikinis."

The doorbell rang. I got up to answer the door, still looking back at Grandma and her mildly dismissive look. Her face went rigid as I opened the door casually, her eyes widening.

I turned. Winter stood inside the doorframe, looking dapper in a light blue suit and white collared shirt, big smile on his face.

"May I come in for a moment?" he said.

I hesitated. "Sure, come on in."

He marched straight to Grandma. "Iris Van Lanen," he said, bringing her hand to his lips. "A great pleasure. As always."

Grandma blushed. "Magistrate Winter, aren't you gallant as ever? What brings you to my granddaughter's doorstep? Good news, I hope."

She had punched the *granddaughter* part, marking her territory.

"It is my duty and honor to keep Sophie safe," Winter assured her.

Gram arched her eyebrows. "Your duty? Is it not our debt?"

"The debt passed down from your ancestor has been re-paid in full. I am now the one who is indebted to you lovely ladies."

Winter turned his attention to Nanya who sat quietly in Gram's lap.

"A borgo," he said. "How peculiar. I didn't know they still existed."

"Thanks to the care they've received in the Deep Down nursery," Gram informed him. "You see, the witch kind are the bearers of life and guardians of all living things. Your kind should take a page from us."

Gram was lecturing the Shadow Warrior.

Precious, Gram, just precious.

"I have always respected your candor, Iris."

"Magistrate, you have always been a gentleman, showing

good intentions towards our family. Yet, when Sophie visited for the holidays, she was quite upset over a fallout you two had. She felt you had deceived her. I trust you will not make her feel that way again."

Somebody kill me now.

"Gram," I said. "That's overstepping. I'm an adult."

Winter grinned. "Not at all, she has every right, Sophie. And, Iris, I can promise you, I will not dare displease Sophie again. She can be as intimidating as her grandmother."

What an ass kisser.

"Okay then," Gram said. "I'll freshen up so you two can talk."

Gram took her bag to the bathroom and closed the door. Water started running in the tub.

Winter put his hands in his pockets. He glanced at me sideways as if he had something to say but wasn't quite sure how to begin. Well, if he came here hoping for the hot action he didn't get last night, it wasn't happening.

"Maybe we can talk later?" I told him. "Gram's just got here, and we have some girl time to catch up on."

"I'll be brief," he said. "I came to say you were right."

"Oh? This is interesting. About what?"

He licked his lips. "You should go to Sweden, Luna, live the life you've planned to live. You in no way, shape or form are ready to face Horror, or Chaos for that matter, and you won't be for centuries. Lie low, explore your possibilities, learn, be your own person. The world is only fresh to us once."

I heard but I didn't understand. "You want me to go?"

He nodded. "What you have wanted is what I want now, too."

"And when did you decide this? Last night you asked me to stay, you wanted to sleep on my couch so you could protect me, and now suddenly I'm better off on another continent?"

"Selfish thoughts consumed me, but I see clearly now."

Right. And why was I upset? Wasn't that my plan, what I had always wanted? Didn't I insist over and over that I wanted to experience a normal life far away from the monsters, beasts and demons? Yet, somehow, coming from his lips, it felt like I was being thrown out and forgotten.

"The mist rider in you has been dormant for too long," he went on. "It will take centuries to fully reshape your powers, and even if you manage that, it won't be enough against Horror, not if you don't find your legendary horse."

"So, what you're saying is that horseless I'm useless to you?"

He sighed. "You're acting like a child again. I thought you wanted this."

You didn't think I was a child last night, did you?

Was this the same man who kissed me and hoisted me up into his lap? Last night, I was a woman and an equal. Today I was an immature nobody to be discarded like old news, to be hidden away for centuries.

I began to shake. Magic rose and I pushed it back down. "What about us?" I said.

"I will always be at your disposal. I will alert my contact within the Immortal network of Scandinavia. There will always be eyes watching and they will alert me if my presence is needed."

Was he acting stupid on purpose? "That's so not what I meant, Jonas. You're honestly the one being a child. I'm talking about *us*. Our personal relationship."

I thought I saw a crack in his rigid façade, but it quickly dispersed. "That was a line that we should never have crossed, Luna. We found ourselves in danger, together, it built an intimacy, a shared pathos, but our connection, if pushed too far, would never work. You know that as well as I do."

"I don't know what I know," I said defiantly. "I don't know everything every second of the day. I'm not six billion years old like you. And you are... you're so old and grumpy and way too arrogant. I mean, *wayyyyyyyy* too arrogant! You'd be a toxic boyfriend, like in new and terrible ways of toxic boyfriending. And besides, why would I want to saddle myself with the first Immortal who crossed my path? As no one said ever, there's a lot of Immortals in the sea. Maybe I can date all of them, I have the fucking time."

A vein pulsed in Winter's temple. His stare assumed the pitiless glare of a hungry predator. It unsettled me. He looked at me with monomaniacal focus. He exhaled and the fury in his eyes dissipated. He cleared his throat.

"I'm honestly just honoring your wishes and doing what's best. I hope it's not too difficult for you to accept my concern for your wellbeing."

"I hate to quote Chaos," I said, shaking my head, "but do you ever even hear yourself? Just get out! Go!"

When I pointed at the door, it popped open at my command. I watched until he stepped off the sidewalk and crossed the street. A woman waited for him by a fence, tall and slim, dressed in tight faded jeans and a burnt orange leather jacket—Kirsi.

The smoking hot sidepiece. Of course.

I was so furious I'd have blown up the apartment if Gram wasn't busy taking a bath. Only last night he had burst through the night sky, looming over Lucia's neighborhood, bouncing from roof to roof like a beautiful demon to get my attention. He had hired people to fix my apartment and had paid my lease for a full year. He had asked me to stay with him. *Bullshit.* All of it.

All those magnificent gestures orchestrated perfectly to sweep the naïve girl off my feet and, my god, how I fell for it. I came that close to letting him do anything he wanted for crying out loud. And I mean, *anything.*

He and Kirsi must be having a good chuckle. Well, screw him.

"Is everything all right, my darling?" Gram said.

I pulled Winter's trick and calmed down my features.

"Yes, Gram," I said. "Everything's perfect as a peach."

NOTHING WAS PERFECT. AND I hated peaches (not really). It was after midnight and I tossed and turned on the couch, unable to sleep. I squeezed the blanket and hissed under my breath. I had let my guard down, I had been a total girl about things, but the sky wasn't falling.

In a way, Winter had set me free. Since our first meeting at the park four months ago, it was the first time I could think about the future and not feel like I was faking it. I should be happy enough about that, but something told me this wasn't where the story ended. There were things Winter wasn't sharing.

Careful not to wake up Gram who was sleeping in my bed, I slipped into my jeans, snatched up my sneakers and tiptoed my way to the door.

The night sky was clear, the moon looked like a half-eaten apple. I called an uber for La Jolla and waited, going over everything in my head.

I had overreacted, there was no denying that. There was also no denying I had been through a traumatic week that had taken an emotional toll. Maybe I could cut myself some slack and, maybe, extend that to Winter.

Standing on the sandy sidewalk below Winter's condo, I watched the waves of the Pacific Ocean lapping onto the beach just a few feet away.

My lungs filled with the salty sea air.

There was a light on somewhere in the condo, probably the kitchen. I took a step toward the gate when the balcony door above opened. Winter stepped out and crossed his arms on the railing. Jazz music thumped from inside. A string of twinkling Christmas lights burst to life along his railing.

A woman stepped next to Winter. Her long, blonde hair fell down her shoulders and back in cascades.

Chazona, the Immortal ice queen who, I was sure, had pursued him throughout the ages of man.

She wrapped her slender arm around his shoulder and whispered into his ear. He laughed.

I stepped behind a palm tree, shielding myself and my shame.

Winter said something and Chazona nodded in agreement. She kissed his cheek. They both laughed. I had seen more than enough.

A second before I turned to go, Chazona threw both arms around his powerful neck. She spun him so his back was to me. Her lips found his and then she gazed down at me, her eyes finding mine in the lamplight.

Her blue eyes narrowed and gleamed with satisfaction, like her whole body was amused by me. She was telling me she had won.

I'm the classic fool.

I marched away, head hung, wishing I had remembered

my jacket. For one fleeting moment, I had wanted to let Winter into my life, to take a side once and for all, form a real bond, a relationship even. Anything to stop me from battling through a thousand scenarios in my head about how I would end up making the wrong choice, and, if there was any truth in Celia's prophecy, how I would screw up and watch the world go up in flames of Horror.

And maybe I was attracted to him despite all his flaws, but what woman wouldn't be? He knew exactly how to draw you in, how to seduce anything that walked on two legs. And to truly judge me, you'd have to kiss him first. We'd see if there was any good sense left in any girl after that.

The intimate moment on the balcony could be a Chazona-style setup, I realized that. She might have seen me and mapped out that scenario. But I also could not fail to see it for what it was—a wakeup call.

I was in no way ready to take sides, let alone allow a three-thousand-year-old Chief Magistrate and Shadow Warrior, superb at killing and manipulation, into my life, my heart and my bed, just because he was hot and made me feel safe for a minute inside an Eternal Vault.

As far as I was concerned, both Chaos and Winter were lethal and loyal only to their own causes. I had a problem with men, you see. I tended to want to believe in them, make excuses for them, give them chance after chance to show their noble essence, their true colors, their ultimate worth.

Maybe it was time I gave myself that chance.

Chapter 25

TWO MONTHS LATER

STOCKHOLM

Göran caught up with me as I was exiting the lecture hall after Professor Lundberg's overlong lecture on traditionality and modernity. My real supernatural power was keeping my eyes open when that man talked.

"Have you snagged a partner for the research project yet?" Göran said.

"Not yet," I said. "I had my sights set on Elsa."

"Oh, no, pick me, pick me," he said as he danced a little jig around me.

I shook my head. "No thanks, you're too manic. A ferret on crack is more chill than you. Hashtag Facts. Hashtag

Tough Love."

"C'mon, Sophie, I'm failing this course and I'm willing to overlook the fact that you're one of those ghastly hashtag people. You know you were put on this Earth to help more charming people than yourself. You know this."

I sighed. I liked Göran. He was cute with an infectious smile and loads of positive energy, but he was also surprisingly lazy for a grad student. "Fine," I said, "but you have to pull your own weight and it has to be a flirt free zone."

"Done and done," he said. "Meet me at Pharmarium tonight?"

I rolled my eyes. "We have to work, Göran, not go out for lagers."

"It's cool. I'll bring the books and everything."

"I'll think about it."

He kissed my cheek and strolled off. I was already regretting my decision to partner up with him. I'd end up doing all the work myself, I just knew it.

At the bus station, I took out my phone to read Lily's latest messages.

> *Need 2 visit u. Stagnation setting in, ugh.*

> *When? I need dates.*

I pondered the perfect reply to my favorite hot mess.

"My homeland favors you," a female voice said. "You're thriving."

I looked up to find Kirsi, Guard of the Seventh Council Seal and Winter's BFF/protégé/sidepiece, grinning at me.

She took a step back and sized me up. "Your aura is dazzling."

"Kirsi, why are you here?"

A young couple walked past. Kirsi asked them something in Swedish. They answered and walked away, waving goodbye at her.

"How's your Swedish?" Kirsi said. "Do you know what I asked them?"

I nodded. "You asked where we could find the best blood pudding."

Kirsi crossed her arms. "Oh yes, I did, it's been a while."

"Well, don't let me keep you," I said.

She bent her face. "Luna, I didn't travel all the way to Stockholm to have blood pudding. I want to talk to you."

I had zero desire to have a conversation with Kirsi. Zero.

"Fine," I said. "But no blood puddings or blood sausages. There's a coffee house around the corner."

She laughed. "Weak stomach?"

I shrugged. "I wasn't around during the days of Viking savagery."

Okay, maybe I shouldn't shit on their history.

The cafeteria patio was built on top of thick logs floating on the Lake Mälaren waters. Most of Stockholm was near water as the city was built on separate islands, connected by fifty-seven bridges.

Despite the chilly weather, several rugged souls were having coffee on the patio. The logs underneath our feet swayed ever so slightly. It felt like we were on a boat.

"To what do I owe the pleasure?" I said.

A solemn expression took over her face. "Luna, on behalf of the Society of Immortal Sisterhood and the Order of Peace Fighters, we would like to extend you an open invitation to join our ranks. We consider you a kindred spirit."

I blinked. "I have no idea what you just said."

Kirsi rubbed her coffee cup. "I belong to a small band of female Immortals who have vowed to support the members of their sisterhood and fight for peace among all supernatural creatures. We'd like to count you as one of us, or at least an honorary member."

Um, okay, this is completely random.

"Well, thanks, I guess, but I'm more of a loner."

Kirsi exhaled. "I get that you're mad. I'm not sure why you're mad at me, exactly, but that whole mess you went through was rough, I get that. Luna, you need real friends, friends who know what you're going through and what you will go through. Let us stand by your side. Sisters in the fight for peace."

"Kirsi, I'm sorry. My life is simple here. I'm enjoying an academic life among the basics and their silly, manageable problems. Frankly, I need a break, a long and distant break from everything magic right now."

She stared ahead into the busy street behind my back. "The city we're in was built on fourteen islands," she said, pensively, "but no being is an island. Immortal or mortal, sooner or later, we all need to know where we stand and who has our back. Do you know how I became a Valkyrie?"

I shook my head. I was actually kind of interested.

"I was born in 928 in a Viking settlement on the east side of the Baltic sea that is now part of Latvia. I never knew my parents. I grew up as an orphan, eating whatever scraps the settlers could spare. I starved to death again and again, only I would magically revive every time. I didn't know I was Immortal until two warrior maidens, Herja and Sigrún, found me asleep on a riverbank when I was six."

"Valkyries," I said.

Kirsi nodded. "Immortals. They knew what I was, so they took me away with them, brought me to Sweden, they dressed me, fed me and trained me. They made me into Kirsi. The two Valkyries formed their own Order within the Immortal network and advocated peace among magic factions at a time when their Immortal male counterparts only cared about war and power and fornicating. These are my sisters and they can be yours too."

I sipped my coffee. "I was a bit terse before. I don't know why, but I will think about your kind offer and I will let you know."

"You do that. If you accept, there'll be a proper reception

for you, and they will cook up ancient delicacies like you've never known."

"I think you just want the cakes," I teased. "Me joining the sisterhood is just your path to those cakes."

She grabbed her heart. "Don't make me deny that. Let's call it 50/50 on my true motivation for your presence in the order."

It was nice to see her after all. I breathed inside my palms trying to warm my hands. "I'm still struggling with the cold weather."

Kirsi considered me a long while. "Speaking of cold weather—"

"What is that look?"

"Winter has feelings for you, Luna, I hope you know that."

I nearly spat out my coffee. How did we go from discussing the lovely independent women peace fighters and cakes to some old magistrate's supposed feelings for the new girl?

Patriarchy anyone?

"What does he know about love?" I said, looking out at the green lake waters. "Do Immortals even experience love after so many years?"

Kirsi grinned. "You think we can't—no, wait, you think *I* can't?"

"Well, can you? Have you ever taken a husband? Have you had a family in all those years you've been alive?"

Her features hardened. "This isn't about me," she said. "His feelings are sincere, Luna. He hasn't felt this way for a woman in a long time."

"Really? And he shared that with you?"

"No, of course not. He doesn't share his inner life. I can see it."

"What about Chazona?"

"Chazona? She never had his heart and she never will."

"Yeah, but I bet she had other parts of him."

Kirsi raised her brows. "Ah, you're jealous?"

I dismissed the notion with a wave of my hand. "Magistrate Winter will never love anyone as much as himself or his plans. And that's a fact."

"That's quite harsh, perhaps born of pain."

"Don't analyze me, Kirsi. Harsh or not, it's accurate."

Kirsi crossed her arms. "I'm not here to convince you of anything. Just keep an open mind. And you shouldn't worry. He has security on you through the local council."

"Is that supposed to make me feel better that Winter has his own stalker network? Proving that he'd rather control me from afar than be here?"

"Why are you so mad at him?"

"I'm not. This is about me. I'm mad at me. Do you understand? All my delusions, my schoolgirl hopes that pull me under time and again."

"Okay, now you're preaching to the choir," Kirsi said, raising her cup to me before taking a sip.

"He couldn't wait to get rid of me, if I'm being honest," I said, then took a sip. "And then he hooked up with Chazona."

She considered my words. "I find that hard to believe."

"You don't have to, girlfriend. I saw it with my own eyes, which is a good thing. I caught a break. Now I'm free and I love my life here. No looking back."

"Fair enough," she said with a sweet smile. "That's great."

It really was. I was moving on. "There's one thing I wanted to ask."

"Fire away," Kirsi said.

"It's about Chaos. I'm strangely drawn to him each time he's about to rush into battle. I don't mean sexually, more like I should be fighting by his side."

She furrowed her brow. "I don't know," she said. "Maybe he's doing that on purpose, using his powers of suggestion. Be careful, Luna, he tried to kill me twice. Once because I defended Winter and another time because I touched his sword. He's full-on crazy."

"You touched his sword?"

We glanced at each other and laughed, our shoulders shaking.

"If he shows up, whatever you do, don't look intimidated," Kirsi warned once she stopped laughing. "Shadows sniff out fear because they're predators and they know how to turn it against you."

"Will do. And, Kirsi, I'm actually glad you came."

I was. There weren't many women like us. I might consider joining that sisterhood club with the delicious cakes.

"I'll go now, but you stay right here."

"What? Why?" I said.

She had such a mischievous smile. "Look over there, Luna."

I glanced in the direction she had pointed. Celia Trice stood inside the cafeteria's main door, in a dark woolen coat and scarf, smiling at us.

I put two and two together. Kirsi was Celia's faithful herald, the person who had informed her of my involvement in the metamorphic night.

Whatever truly brought Celia to my new home must be very serious.

Kirsi squeezed my hand and took off, leaving her chair to Celia.

Faion's grandmother cupped my hand in hers. "So lovely to meet again much sooner than we thought, my dear," she said.

I almost didn't want to ask. "Do you have news for me? How's Faion?"

She leaned forward. "Indeed, I do, and Faion is as always, having too much fun. Do not worry, my news is not unbearable."

That didn't sound as reassuring as she thought. I couldn't help it, I became impatient. "Did you divine my origins? Or who gave me to Winter?"

"No," she said. "That which I reveal today will not bring further clarity to you, child. The path to enlightenment ventures in and out of darkness as it goes winding along."

I've been on that path a while.

"I will always choose the light," I said. "I'm done with Shadows and their murky ways."

Celia sat back to open her purse. She took out one of her cigarette-shaped gums. "The choice isn't always between light and dark, Luna. Not in the basic world. Not in our world. We all have our own shade of reality."

"And that's what you came all this way to tell me?"

Celia took a deep breath. I had never seen the grand lady one bit anxious before, not until this very moment. "The Shadow known as Chaos, you and he share the same blood."

I smiled because that was literally true. "He gave me a blood transfusion, Celia. That doesn't mean we're going to exchange gifts at Christmas."

She was not amused. She looked into my eyes with a Grandma's concern.

"What?" I said. "You're trying to say he's related to me somehow?"

"I feel a blood connection, and it is strong."

Yeah, no way. Wires crossed. Diviner Wi-Fi down.

"Did you hear what I said, Ms. Celia? Back in January, Chaos donated some of his blood to help me heal. That's it. That's all you're picking up."

"My sweet Luna, only an Immortal blood relative can

match your blood."

The world came racing in on me.

"You mean, both Winter and Chaos knew Chaos is related to me?"

Celia did not answer. She didn't need to.

Motherf—I stopped. Even swearing in my head was not cool in front of Faion's grandmother.

"I can't be his relation," I said. "We're not even the same thing."

Celia shrugged. "Stranger things have happened in heaven and hell and all the realms between. Immortals mating with mortals and every other possible mix. Love and desire are boundless, the uncontained magic. There are even cases where the blood relation is artificial, as in the case of a predestined coupling in infancy where blood is exchanged between the infants to bond them for life. A very archaic and rare practice but not unheard of and that's the tip of the iceberg of possibilities."

She had one thing right at least. This brought me no clarity. In fact, if she had rubbed mud in my eyes, that would have been better.

"How related could we be? He's thousands of years older."

"I don't have answers," Celia said, "but there is someone who can look into the past for you." She paused, locking her eyes on mine. "She always asks for a price, Luna, and that price will not be an easy price to pay, whatever it will be. Such knowledge comes at a substantial cost."

And there it was, another awful choice looming. I could ignore what Celia said and keep on with my nearly idyllic life as a graduate student, or I could risk everything to uncover the mystery of who and what I was.

When you live forever, reality will always catch up with you.

"Luna," Celia said, "I am here, whatever you choose."

A group of students stepped onto the floating patio, gesticulating and talking loudly. I recognized two of them from a party I'd been to last week. I'd watched them get drunk while I pretended to be tipsy.

My life was absurd, even when at a basic party. I looked at my feet, remembered buying these shoes with Lil.

My vision blurred. Blood thumped in my ears.

"Yeah, let's do it. Arrange a meeting, Celia," I said. "It's not like it wouldn't happen eventually. Might as well do it now. Let me know when and where."

I stood and glanced across the water at a woman hanging her knickers outside a third-floor window. She had a white ribbon in her hair.

My idyllic life suddenly felt like a terrible ruse, a deception of self. All that I had lost was my innocence. I had to accept it. I had to accept that I was a mist rider and that I had embarrassing Immortal relatives.

I'm not the first girl who ever had to endure embarrassing relatives.

The final battle for a free Earth lay out there somewhere on the Eternal path, a path that winds and never ends, a path I can never escape.

Now is when I stop running.

About the Author

Stella Fitzsimons was born in Athens, Greece, and lives in Southern California with her husband and two sons. After studying economics and language arts she went on to teach both Mathematics and English before launching *Stella's Literary Bistro*, a bilingual literary journal. Her works include: *The Vanishing Tome, Luna, Winter, Silver Dust, Shadow Fall, Moonlight Mist* and *The Last Rider.*